AFTER THE RIDE

CRIME AND COMPASSION

J.R. Conway
2/10/2023

J.R. CONWAY

BookVenture Publishing LLC
1000 Country Lane Ste 300
Ishpeming MI 49849
www.bookventure.com
Hotline: 1(877) 276-9751
Fax: 1(877) 864-1686

Ordering Information:
Quantity sales. Special discounts are available on quantity purchases by corporations, associations, and others. For details, contact the publisher at the address above.

Printed in the United States of America.

Library of Congress Control Number		2018936810
ISBN-13:	Softcover	978-1-64166-663-3
	Hardcover	978-1-64166-664-0
	Pdf	978-1-64166-665-7
	ePub	978-1-64166-666-4
	Kindle	978-1-64166-667-1

Rev. date: 03/03/2018

This book is dedicated to Faride (Foddy) Conway, my wife of thirty-one years. It was her encouragement that set my literary effort in motion. May she rest in peace.

PROLOGUE

A sequel to the book entitled *Greyhound Therapy,* a fictional treatment of the impact on small communities when people move from one jurisdiction to another by bus. Authorities and mental health institutions sometimes find it more economical or convenient to furnish individuals with a bus ticket rather than, for whatever reason, meet their needs.

JR Conway's previous book, *Greyhound Therapy,* introduces the reader to some of the problems that could arise when troubled individuals or persons with criminal intent arrive in the small town of Rock Springs, Wyoming, by bus. The greatest impact falls on law enforcement. The sheriff, Craig Spence, though undermanned and having insufficient resources, is tasked with dealing with an influx of such arrivals, exasperated by conditions resulting from a gas and oil boom.

In *Greyhound Therapy* Conway takes the reader on a thrilling, fast-moving series of events that makes it difficult to put the book down. The protagonist, Sheriff Spence solicits the help of a local security company to augment his force, something few—if any—law enforcement agencies would do, while he dealt with a murder in his own jail, navigated the politics that is prevalent in most county governments and directed a multi-force effort to chase and apprehend a depraved killer. All the while, Sheriff Spence labors at his job knowing he could lose his wife who has been diagnosed with cancer.

Most of the transients that arrive in Rock Springs on the bus are homeless and petty criminals who find themselves least exposed to detection when traveling by bus. A great number, however, are persons that have been shipped from jurisdictions across the country because it's far away or because of the probability that a job can be found in an oil or gas-related industry is high. Then there are those who are emotionally or mentally unstable, are out of prescribed medications for their conditions, who engage in undesirable behavior resulting in their becoming deemed a danger to themselves and others. Being so deemed they become wards of Craig Spence, and are confined against their will.

Occasionally, persons damaged by war, and set afloat in an environment in which they are no longer equipped to function, end up as wards of Sheriff Spence. While this book addresses the probabilities of just such a case, it also answers many of the reader's questions regarding people and events left unanswered in *Greyhound Therapy* and again, Conway takes the reader through a thrilling minefield of crime and mystery.

CHAPTER

The bus began to pick up speed as it traversed the on ramp to I-25 North out of Denver, Colorado. It was the evening rush hour and the driver deftly merged into the traffic. The total travel time for this trip to Salt Lake City, Utah, would be approximately twelve hours with stops in Laramie, Rock Springs, and Evanston, Wyoming. Glancing in the interior rearview mirror, all his passengers seemed to be settled in for the ride. The bus was almost full. Only a few seats were unoccupied.

There was a small group of students headed for the University of Wyoming at Laramie. It was the month of March and from his years of driving this route, he surmised that they had been on spring break, were tuckered out and heading back to begin the next semester of classes. There were a dozen or so unaccompanied males, some dressed in coveralls and welder's caps or bandanas tied around their heads. Others wore Western-styled hats with wide red or black ribbons around the crowns. All had transferred from the express out of Oklahoma City. They all stowed tool boxes in the compartments below and were headed for Evanston, Wyoming, where a major oil company had a man camp at which its employees were housed. They regularly hired hands from all over the country through an employment agency and if they didn't have their own transportation, they would be provided vouchers to travel either by air or by bus. He recalled that many of his passengers today were singles with very little baggage. In the last few months there had been many riders, male and female, heading to Wyoming looking for work in the industries generated by the oil and natural gas boom. There were also several elderly people on board that appeared to be tourist. Each had several pieces of luggage and boxes that looked as though they were gifts. One middle-aged gentleman had no baggage at all, and he was traveling on a voucher. The driver had taken special notice of him because he stood off to the side and didn't board until everyone else had. He approached the door with a limp and the driver noticed he wore his cap pulled way down on his head. His only carry-on was a blue cloth grocery bag and he took a seat at the rear of the bus.

Remnants of a recent snowstorm lined the sides of the highway and as the bus left the metropolitan areas, the fields were still dressed in a light coating of snow that had an orange hue, reflecting the light from the setting sun, only half now visible on the horizon, casting its last light upon individual swaths of cirrus clouds that stretched across the evening sky. The clicking of cameras could be heard as the passengers tried to capture what is seldom seen in other parts of the country. Once the sun was gone and darkness fell, silence, too, settled in as the bus crossed the Colorado border into Wyoming, and connected with I-80 West to Laramie, Rock Springs, Evanston, and Salt Lake.

It was after 2:00 a.m. when the bus pulled up to a modified double wide mobile home that was the arrival and departure point in Laramie. "This is Laramie, folks," the driver announced over the intercom. "I'll unlock the double doors. Once inside, the restrooms will be to your left. I advise you to take advantage of this break since Rock Springs is a little over three hours from here. We'll be stopped here for exactly twenty minutes. Don't be late," he cautioned. Everyone heeded his advice except the gentleman in the rear of the bus. He just stayed in his seat clutching his bag and really appeared to be uncomfortable, the driver thought.

During the evening and early morning hours truckers tried to make as much distance as possible. The evenings and early morning hours were generally without the constant winds that Wyoming is known for. The trucks were traveling in convoys of six or more and the ribbons of light could be seen for miles ahead. The bus driver kept the bus in the inside lane and easily passed the groups of trucks and maintained a steady seventy-five miles per hour.

The silence was abruptly broken by a loud *pow* followed by *bloop, bloop, bloop* and stuff striking the side of the bus.

"Incoming!" Someone shouted from the rear of the bus.

Through his right outside mirror the driver could see that a tire on the trailer of the truck he was passing had blown and it was disintegrating, flinging pieces of rubber against the side of the bus. There was a lot of yelling and screaming going on toward the back of the bus so he turned up the interior lighting. Two female passengers were standing in their seats, clutching each other. He could see a pair of legs sticking out into the aisle, and one of the male passengers was attempting to grab them but was being kicked repeatedly. Over the intercom the driver inquired. "What's going on back there?"

"We've got a crazy trying to stuff himself under the seats," was the reply.

"Does he seem to be in any physical distress? Breathing okay?"

"He's shaking and muttering something about being killed by his own people."

"Unless he shows signs that he's having difficulty breathing, let him be. Keep an eye on him. You, ladies, find other seats. We'll be where we can get him some help shortly," the driver advised.

*****

The journey for Kenneth Boutros from a healthy, stable young man in his midtwenties, to this middle-aged person seeking cover between the seats, started many years prior when he served as a helicopter door gunner for a defense contractor that was conducting covert operations across the Laotian border during the Vietnam conflict. It was while returning from one of those operations that Kenneth's life would change forever.

The pilots had just spotted a marine forward fire base on top of a ridge—they always used it as a visual navigational checkpoint—when the front of the chopper was decimated by something, probably a rocket propelled grenade (RPG). Their flight path was too close to the side of the hills and some Viet Cong (VC) soldier had gotten lucky.

From the fire base, the craft was seen to crash in an area of the jungle that was known to be occupied by the VC who frequently lobbed mortar rounds into the base. The base commander immediately notified his headquarters of the crash.

The helicopter assumed a nose high attitude as it plummeted and entered the jungle tail first and Kenneth was thrown out upon impact. The tail boom of the craft broke off and what remained of the fuselage came to rest on top of Kenneth, the right skid, pinning his leg at the knee. The pain was excruciating. Any attempts to move sent agonizing bolts of pain through his body. He didn't dare scream even though he knew the VC would be there soon enough. After a time, he had no idea how long after the crash, he'd thought he'd heard voices. All he had was his side arm, a .38-caliber revolver. Just taking it from its holster almost caused him to pass out from the pain.

It seemed like forever before he heard the sound that made him feel that there was a chance that he might make it out. That familiar *whop, whop* sound made by the blades of Huey helicopters. The cavalry was coming. He tried to estimate how many from the sound—four, he thought. As they got closer, he strained to look up through the hole the chopper's blades had made when it fell through the trees, to get a glimpse of those magnificent birds. One flew right over the hole, a Charlie model gunship, only visible for a fleeting moment. Then he heard the machine gun fire and bullets were ricocheting into the wreckage above him, tearing out large pieces of metal. *Those rounds were hitting dammed close,* he thought. The VC must have been closing in. *God,* he thought, *am I going to be killed by my own people?* Then the jungle exploded around the crash site as the gunships fired rockets into the dense foliage. That's all Kenneth remembers. He didn't see the arrival of a five-man patrol sent from the fire base, nor did he see the brown helicopter with the big Red Cross on the front swoop in and slowly come to a hover just above the wreckage. A ricochet or shrapnel had taken a chunk out of his flight helmet and a portion of his upper forehead with it.

With a metal plate in his head and a tendency to be violent, Kenneth spent most of the past several years on the street, in and out of one jail or another, and finally in a state mental institution in northern Colorado. During treatment sessions, counselors learned that Kenneth had relatives in Farson, Wyoming. With the help of the Sweetwater County Public Records Department, contact was made with Bruce Boutros, the owner of a sheep ranch located west of the town of Farson. Bruce Boutros agreed that when Kenneth was ready to be released, he could come and live on the ranch. That was a little over six months prior to this bus trip. All attempts to contact Bruce since had failed but the mental health facility could no longer keep Kenneth hospitalized. He was given a voucher and a three-day supply of medication and put on a bus.

CHAPTER

Craig Spence, the longtime sheriff of Sweetwater County, had gotten to his office early as usual in preparation for a staff meeting with his supervisory personnel—his jail administrator, Sherrie Munson; Steve Lolly, his second-in-command plus patrol supervisor; and his chief investigator, Kevin Marcy. This being a Monday, everyone would be giving briefings and updates on their department's operations, and as usual, Sherrie was the first to arrive.

"Good morning, Sheriff," she pleasantly greeted him. "Looks like we might have a nice day," she related alluding to the fact that the sun was shining for the first time in weeks.

"Hi ya, Sherrie! I detect a melodic tone in your voice this morning, was that brought on by the weather?"

"For the first time in months, this weekend I got out of town. I got rid of a lot of stress. I do feel refreshed."

"Date?" he asked.

"Ummm, sorta," she said tilting her head and pursing her lips.

"Good for you," Craig said.

Steve and Kevin hurried into the room as if they thought they were late. Craig checked his watch and sure enough it was 7:35 and the meeting was scheduled to start at 7:30.

"Now that we're all here," Craig began, pausing for emphasis. "I know you all would like to know how Martha's doing. Last night, since we don't have a dog house, she threatened to have me move into one of the jail cells if I didn't get from under foot."

"She's coming along," Steve quipped.

"That's a good sign," Craig continued, "tomorrow she starts her radiation treatments and I'm hoping that goes well." He cleared his throat and pulled a pad of paper in front of him. "For the next couple of days, I'm going to be busy with the county attorney preparing for the ACLU hearings," Craig informed them. "As you know, the county and I have been named in a suit because of conditions in the jail. We've come up with a plan that may forestall this lawsuit by the ACLU from going to trial. For the next couple of days, unless it's something to do with budgets or legal, you handle it, Steve, and brief me at the end of the day. Sherrie, how did we fair over the weekend?"

"This was not a bad weekend. Only drunks that were disorderly ended up being held over for court appearances today. Early this morning we did get a call from the Rock Springs police that they were taking an individual to emergency detention at the hospital. He came in on the bus and had some type of issue that caused him to be put off and taken into custody. Dispatch requested the security company to furnish a guard at the hospital. Hiring them on was a great decision on your part, Sheriff. They've saved us numerous man hours." Sherrie paused for a moment while she removed some papers from a brown envelope. She passed a sheet to the rest of the staff and to Craig, and then she continued. "The name of the party committed is Kenneth Boutros. He gave this letter to the officers. It's from a Colorado state mental institution in Ft. Morgan, Colorado. I'll give you a moment to read it."

COLORADO
Mental Treatment Center
Ft. Morgan, Colorado

To Whom It May Concern:

This letter introduces Mr. Kenneth Boutros who has been in the care of this institution where he has been treated for psychological and behavioral disorders. Kenneth is prone to have instances of violent behavior that are usually triggered by stressful situations, unexpected loud noises, or physical confrontation.

Approximately six months ago, contact was made with a relative, Mr. Bruce Boutros, who resides in Farson, Wyoming off county road 28, who consented and agreed to allow Mr. Kenneth Boutros to reside with him upon completion of treatment and subsequent release from this facility (a copy of letter affirming the arrangement is attached). Treatment at this institution has been completed and it is not in the best interest of Kenneth to be released on his own, back on the street.

Recent efforts to recontact Mr. Bruce Boutros have not been successful. Kenneth has been instructed to present this letter to local police, church organizations, health care facilities, etc., and seek help in connecting with his relatives.

For any additional information regarding Mr. Kenneth Boutros, it is recommended that you reach his counselor, Mr. Delano Petreti, at this institution.

Delano Petreti
Colorado Mental Treatment Center

"Does anyone know this Bruce Boutros?" Sherrie asked.

"Old man Boutros ran sheep on several hundred acres of ranch land in the Eden Valley, west of Farson, for over sixty years," Craig spoke up. "He passed away several months back and I had a sheriff's sale to payoff back taxes. We sold the sheep, all the equipment, sheepherder's wagons, and most of the ranch land. I recall some outfit out of Kemmerer, owned by a relative, paid the taxes. The old man's wife passed years ago. I specifically remember though that there was no telephone service to the ranch. All communications out there was done by radio. We sold those too. You might check with the clerk or assessor's office, see who the owners are now."

"I thought also that I'd have Ted Harper, the deputy in Farson, go out there and contact whomever," Sherrie said. Everyone agreed that she should follow through on that idea. "There was also some movement on the situation with the nun that is in emergency detention," Sherrie continued. "Sister Patricia Ann had been found by a bus driver west of Green River, curled up in the middle of the highway nearly frozen to death and noncommunicative. The county court held a hearing on Friday," Sherrie was saying. "The doctor in charge of Patricia's care partitioned the court for authority to have a neurological workup done. He felt that based on observations of her behavior, there was something very serious going on with her, but in the absence of any medical history, he recommended that exams be done as soon as possible. The court ordered that Sister Patricia Anne be held in detention for an additional seven days and that the medical staff proceed with a neurological workup. Patricia didn't attend the hearing because her condition has continued to worsen. She was represented by an attorney from the public defender's office. On behalf of Patricia the attorney consented to the court's decision."

"Has there been any effort by anyone to contact the sisters of the Sacred Heart?" Craig inquired of Sherrie. The nun belonged to that order located in Dayton, Wyoming.

"Yes, sir," Sherrie responded. "We contacted Sheridan County Sheriff, Don Thatcher, who spoke with the Reverend Mother at the nunnery and he faxed information over the weekend and I've only glanced at it, but apparently, Patricia left Dayton the day she was picked up on the highway, to go to Ft. Bridger to fill in for the regular administrative assistant at St. Joseph's Catholic Church."

"Didn't anyone get concerned when she didn't show up?" Craig asked.

"Didn't get that far into the report yet, Sheriff," Sherrie advised. "As soon as I get back to my office I'll go through it and get back with you."

"I may not be here," Craig reminded. "Steve, follow-up on this and get as many answers as you can. I want to know what happened to that little lady."

"You bet, boss," Steve acknowledged.

"What else you got, Sherrie?" Craig inquired.

"That's it, Sheriff."

"Okay, Kevin, I see you're still pretty gimpy on that leg. How's it doing?" Kevin had taken a bullet to the leg during an encounter with an escaped murderer a week or so ago.

"It's pretty sore," Kevin said. "Just have to be careful not to start it bleeding. I can be just as careful here as I could if I were home."

"You don't leave this office, understand?" Craig directed. "Besides the pain in that leg, what's gonna keep you up at night this week?"

"We've made progress on the stolen brass bushing from Sweetwater Coal Mine," Kevin began. "We now know that it was an inside job, we know when it left the mine and we know what truck outfit hauled it off. What we don't know yet is who the inside guy is. There is some indication that this may be the work of a group that has been hitting several of the mines for copper cabling. The Utah people are working on this from their end because that's where the trucking company is from."

"How'd you find all this out?" Craig asked with excitement in his voice.

"The mine property and the power plant are only separated by a chain-link fence. Instead of taking the thing out of the main gate of the mine, someone let the truck through an access gate in the fence to the railhead at the power plant. When the truck exited through the power plant's main gate the security people there logged the truck out and made a note as to what was on it. They received a phone call from the night superintendent's office okaying the truck's departure without the usual paper work."

"So, what's your next move?" Craig continued to show interest.

"There had to be a good-sized piece of equipment used to handle that bushing. A cherry picker or hoist to get it off the warehouse floor and loaded onto the truck. Every employee at the mine belongs to the union out there. According to the security people, union rules prohibit a circuit breaker being reset unless it's done by an electrician, so any equipment used was probably operated by a heavy equipment operator. The official responsible for security at the mine is going through logs and sign-in sheets and such to determine who was on duty that night and would have been the equipment operator and what supervisor might have cleared that truck to leave the property."

"Speaking of unions," Craig interjected, "a union representative will probably be present when you conduct any interviews or interrogations on mine property. This is not always a bad thing but it could complicate things. Just be aware."

"My plan is to contact any probable participants or witnesses in locations and settings where they will feel the least intimidated."

"Very good," Craig concurred. "Besides being my backup, Steve, you had any movement on your projects?"

"Boss, I've got some good news and some bad news," he began. "The good news is we found Patricia's car. The highway patrol located it on state Highway 372, twenty-eight miles east of the National Wildlife Refuge and four miles west of Green River. The window in the driver's door was shattered, the interior was trashed, a suitcase of clothing had been dumped and the contents of a purse was strewn all over the front seats and floor. No ID or credit cards were found. The registration information was in the clove compartment. The bad news, there was no medications found. It had been hoped that there would have been some medications in the car so that the doctors would know what she could have possibly been being treated for."

"Where is the car now?" Craig asked.

"The car was towed to Little America Hotel and Truck Stop just west of Green River. I'll have our guys pick it up and bring it to Green River where we can begin to process it," Steve responded.

"I can't imagine a woman leaving her purse behind," Craig stated. "Unless she was taken or was having a medical episode of some sort."

"An investigator from the Sheridan sheriff's office will be contacting the Mother Superior at the convent today. What Patricia was being treated for and what medications she was taking are questions he'll be looking for answers to," Steve advised.

"Looks like we've all got our work cut out for us so let's get to it," Craig said as he stood and gathered the papers in front of him.

At his desk Craig mulled over some papers in a folder for a few moments then picked up the phone and dialed the number to the county attorney's office.

"County attorney's office, this is Sarah." She'd answered after the second ring.

"Hi ya, Sarah. You're in early this morning," Craig commented. "Looking at a busy day, are ya?"

"Three arraignments, two bond hearings, and jury selection for an upcoming trial next week," she responded. "Oh, and by the way, just got a note that there is going to be a coroner's inquest this week regarding your dispatching of Mr. Brown."

It was Craig that finally took out the escaped murderer that put that bullet in Kevin's leg.

"Isn't that a little unusual?" Craig asked.

"Not really," Sarah responded. "In such cases its best to put a ribbon around the package."

"Okay, but the reason I called is that I've got an idea that might prevent us from having to go to trial on the ACLU lawsuit."

"I'd sure like to hear that, how about after 4:30 today?"

"It's a date, doll, your office after 4:30," Craig confirmed.

Over the weekend Craig and Martha were spending some quite time together, she was sitting on the living room floor, thumbing through some old magazines on the coffee table before she discarded them, and he comfortably nestled in his favorite recliner catching up with the local news in the papers that had piled up during the week.

"I see where the chamber of commerce is considering canceling the fishing derby at the Gorge this year," Craig announced from behind an outstretched paper. "Waters down, rocks and stumps exposed, hazardous to boaters," he continued.

"Heard on the TV that they were even considering moving the

marina on the north end of the lake," Martha responded without looking up from her magazine. "Here's an interesting tidbit. The state of Wyoming distributed $889 of oil and gas revenues to counties last year. Sweetwater County's share was 19.3 million." After a slight pause, she continued. "I wonder what they did with that money."

She had gotten Craig's attention. He folded the newspaper and scooted down on the floor beside her.

"Let me see that," he said as he reached for the magazine. It was the *Wyoming Business Report*, published by the University of Wyoming. The article Martha had referred to was written by a member of the Wyoming oil and gas commission and it broke down all the revenues received by the state, through the taxation process for oil, gas, and trona extraction as well as other minerals. Then it showed how much of that money the state distributed to each county.

"Doll, smartest thing I ever did was to bring you home to Mom, you're worth your weight in gold," he said as he took her face in his hands, rubbed noses, and kissed her on the lips. "I think I might just be able to ward off a lawsuit," he said as he got up and took the magazine to his briefcase.

Martha called after him. "Woo, woo, I like it when you get excited."

Craig was waiting in Sarah's office when she returned from her day in court. While she was returning her files to their places in the appropriate cabinets, he began to speak, "Sarah," he began, "you're a disgrace to your profession."

"What does that mean," she spat out at him, somewhat annoyed.

"Every attorney I've known over the years just kept putting stuff in piles on their desk until they'd run out of room and then they'd start on the floor."

"I was a file clerk for a supreme court judge before passing the bar," she shared. "She did not take kindly to waiting for files. She expected you to have it to her almost before she knew she needed it. Putting them back where they belonged kept me in good stead. Now that you have demonstrated your prowess of observation, what's on your mind?"

Craig took the magazine that he had folded and put in his hip pocket, put it on the desk and turned to the article regarding revenues from oil and gas before speaking. "You and I both know that we're going to take a beating if we go to trial with the ACLU regarding conditions at the jail. To make matters worse, the court will probably dictate when and how we solve the problems and we'll have very little input, if any. The county commissioners don't really care because all they must do is comply with the court's decision, we are going to have to live with whatever is decided. You're the attorney, but I say let's don't go to trial. Here's what I'm thinking."

Craig picked up the magazine and moved where he stood beside Sarah sitting at her desk.

"Last year the county's portion of the state's oil and gas revenue was darn near $20,000,000 to $19.3 million to be exact. I checked with the county treasurer's office and only twenty percent, or a little over three million of that has been spent or encumbered. They haven't met yet to allocate portions of what's left. I say let's get to them before they get set on any ideas and have them allocate a portion of that money to the planning and construction of a new detention center."

Sarah continued reading the article in silence. When she had finished, she scooted her chair back, folded her arms across her chest, and through squinted eyes said to Craig, "I get the feeling you want me to convince the commissioners."

"Well, you are the county attorney," Craig reminded.

"That's exactly why I can't do it. But here's what I can do." She took out a day timer and pointed to some notes before continuing. "The next commissioner's meeting is two weeks from now. I can ask that the hearing that's scheduled for tomorrow be postponed until after that meeting, I'll get you on the agenda and you can make your pitch to the commissioners. You'll also have two weeks to influence any supporters you may have on the commission."

"It's a deal, Sarah, I gather you think there's merit to my idea?"

"Knowing you, I'd say there is a 60/40 chance that we may be able to pull it off. Now get out of here so I can go home," she said with a smile.

CHAPTER

Sister Patricia Anne, the nun that had been lying in the middle of the highway and picked up by a bus driver and turned over to the police, was from an order located in Dayton, Wyoming. The nunnery was a ranch that was willed to the order by a wealthy parishioner, in which the Sisters of the Sacred Heart lived, consisted of a large two-story gray stone house that was their living quarters, contained a chapel, dining facilities, and a laundry, two outbuildings, one of which was a bunkhouse that had been converted to classrooms and used to teach religious classes, a smaller house that was the ranch foreman's quarters that houses lay staff—a cook, several farm hands, and a couple of maintenance people. A large barn that served as storage for equipment, contained stalls for several horses, provided shelter for a small flock of sheep, a herd of twenty or so goats and three Holstein cows.

The sisters were the benefactors of several hundred acres of prime farm land situated in a long valley bordered on both sides by the foothills of the Big Horn mountain range and located four miles north of US Highway 14. During the growing season, all types of vegetables were raised and sold at a roadside stand just outside of the city limits. A large portion of the land was allocated to the planting of hay and alfalfa that was sold to horse owners and ranchers throughout the region.

The Sisters of the Sacred Heart served parishes throughout Wyoming by teaching in summer and parochial schools, providing care for the sick and elderly, and substituting as administrative assistants to churches when there was illness or when regular help is to be absent for extended periods of time. When at the nunnery the daily schedule was routine.

4:00–6:00 a.m.: Prayers
6:00–8:00 a.m.: Divine Liturgy (when all residents come together)
8:00–10:00 a.m.: Breakfast
10:00 a.m.–1:00 p.m.: Work (cleaning, minor maintenance, book keeping, prepare meals, care for the animals, etc.)
1:00–1:30 p.m.: Lunch
1:30–2:00 p.m.: Clean up
2:00–5:00 p.m.: Quiet time
5:00–5:30 p.m.: Vesper prayers
5:30–7:00 p.m.: Quiet time
7:00–7:30 p.m.: Dinner
7:30–8:00 p.m.: Spiritual readings
8:00 p.m.–4:00 a.m.: Quiet time/sleep

*****

When she was at the nunnery, Sister Patricia Anne's chore was to milk the goats, and make sure the kids were healthy and well. When she was assigned to one of the parishes, other nuns would fill in for her. So was the case today. She was leaving to assist with administrative tasks at St. Joseph's church in Ft. Bridger, Wyoming. She had packed her bags into her little Honda Civic, made sure she had her medication in her purse, and a plastic container of water on the floor on the passenger side. She hadn't felt well for about a week, and the doctor in town felt that she may have ammonia problems. She didn't take the medicine today because it makes her drowsy and she can't seem to concentrate afterward. She'd take it after the drive, she thought.

She was dressed for the road. The traditional habit was not worn by the Sisters of the Sacred Heart, they wore suits of navy, black, or grey. When they traveled they could wear what was appropriate for weather conditions. Because the heater in the Civic was not the greatest, Patricia chose to wear sweatpants, a wool shirt along with a navy blue zip-up jacket, and a blue knitted bonnet.

It was a beautiful drive through the foothills of the Big Horn mountain range. State Highway 14 cut high along the hills allowing her to look down upon vast vistas of trees and rock formations that bordered valleys that stretched for miles until they butted against the beginning of a distant set of foothills. At one point, at a sightseeing pull over area, she stopped to watch a group of young people jump off the side of the road and paraglide some distance to the valley floor.

She was a little over four hours into what was to be a six-hour trip when she recognized the first sign of trouble. Her vision became blurry, objects such as fence posts no longer had distinct outlines, and she was beginning to suffer a throbbing headache. Not taking the medicine may not have been a great idea, she thought. She slowed the car and kept saying to herself, *Don't panic, Patricia, don't panic, trust in the lord.*

When she squinted things seemed to come into focus better. She could see the white line on the side of the road, and she followed it, and it finally led her to another scenic overlook. She stopped the car, shut off the engine, and closed her eyes hoping it might help clear her vision. She now realized that she needed to relieve herself bad, but first she'd take that medicine. If she had taken it according to schedule—every six hours—it would be time for the second pill of the day, so she'd just take two now.

There were some pinion trees and some tall grass at the edge of the overlook. She had never gone in bushes before. She would never do such a thing, but this was an emergency. Her headache seemed to be getting worse as she staggered to the bushes. Unfortunately, she hadn't noticed a rock where she squatted and the velocity caused urine to splash all over her shoes.

As she made her way back to the car, she experienced light-headedness. She managed to get her shoes off and put them on the floor, in the back of the car. She'd just sit for a while and let the medicine begin to work, she thought. It was beginning to get cool in the car so she decided to start the car so the heater would warm things up. When she turned the key, nothing happened. She tried several times but nothing happened. She turned the key to the "on" position and turned the radio knob to "on," there was sound but scratchy. She pulled the jacket tight around her neck, pulled her feet up under her, and huddled in the front seat.

The loud rumble of a large oil field service truck going by startled her awake. She had fallen asleep and had no idea for how long. The car windows were fogged over and she wiped the window on the driver's side with her arm so she could see outside. The sun was going down. She felt light-headed, and that headache was still there, and she seemed to be in a fog, she just couldn't think. She noticed the keys in the switch and she stared at them for some time before realizing what they were for. She turned them to start but nothing happened and she just couldn't figure out what to do. Her hands and feet were cold. *Walk,* she thought. Walk to keep her feet warm.

She left the car and began to walk toward some lights that she could see in the distance. Her feet hurt but she kept walking and began to hum the refrain of a song she could remember. As she hummed, the words manifested themselves in her mind.

"To the lost Christ shows his face; to the unloved he gives his embrace; to those who cry in pain or disgrace, Christ, makes, with his friends, a touching place . . ."

Back in her office, Sherrie began to read through the papers Sheriff Don Thatcher had faxed over. On the cover sheet under subject was: "Conversation with Sister Mary Margret." She set it aside and began to read from the second sheet. He had printed the information using a pen and she tried to imagine his personality from the writing style.

Ms. Munson, as requested, I met with Sister Mary Margret at the convent. She was very concerned because she had not heard from Sister Patricia Anne and she had not been able to reach anyone at the rectory at St. Joseph's Parish in Ft. Bridger, where she was going. For the past several weeks Sister Patricia Anne suffered headaches and had had periods when she seemed confused about things. She had seen a doctor and was taking medicine for elevated ammonia and was being treated for the headaches. She had no idea what had been prescribed but it seemed to have helped, the sister said. She had been feeling so much better that when the request for assistance came from Ft. Bridger, she volunteered to go. Just to give you a little background, I've known Sister Patricia Anne and her family since she was a teen. Her name was Clara then. Her mother suffered from alcoholism, went blind, and eventually died of a brain tumor. Her father was a colleague of mine in the Wyoming Highway Patrol. At the age of fifteen, Clara ran away to the convent and her dad was accused and convicted of molesting her. She grew up in the care of the nuns and became a nun herself. By the way, one of my deputies checked with the doctor that is treating the sister but was unable to find out what the medications are. The doctor will tell us if he has the sister's permission. Have her call him at 307-233-8354. If I can be of further service to your department don't hesitate to call. Don.

After passing the information to Steve, Sherrie contacted Ted Harper. Ted had been with the sheriff's office for almost six years now. He lived in Farson and covered all the Eden Valley. Besides the town of Farson, his area consisted mostly of the small village of Eden, ranches, farms, some oil and gas leases, and numerous manufactured homes that were sprinkled throughout the valley. Ted spent most of his time serving legal papers but occasionally he would be called upon by the state game and fish department to assist in the apprehension of subjects suspected of poaching and the illegal taking of wild game. Generally, it's difficult to contact Ted by phone but today she was lucky.

Ted Harper was a chubby young man with chipmunk cheeks, red hair, and an engaging smile. He'd joined the sheriff's department just after his twenty-third birthday, six years ago. He had lived in the Valley all his life and married his high school sweetheart. After graduating from high school, he worked a few years as a ranch hand but when the department advertised the deputy's position in the Valley, Dolly, his wife, encouraged him to apply.

"Deputy Harper, how can I help you?" Ted answered after the third ring.

"Hi, Ted, Sherrie here."

"Hey, babe, what's going on?" Ted answered.

"I need a favor, but first I want to thank you for a great time this weekend."

"It was a nice time, wasn't it? We'll have to do it again sometime."

"I'd like that, Ted," she said.

"What's the favor?"

"We've got a guy in emergency detention that has been released from a mental treatment center in Colorado. Prior to his release, an arrangement was made with Bruce Boutros for him to go live on the ranch. Well, the old man is dead and we need to contact the people who now own the ranch."

"Yeah," Ted cut in. "I remember the sheriff's sale we had out there. I haven't been out there since but I believe some distant relative paid off the taxes and took the place over."

"Would you take a run out there and see if the deal is still good. We can't hold him in detention much longer. Let me know what you find out as soon as you can."

"I'll do that first thing, Sherrie. Should be back with you in a couple of hours. You have a nice day now."

"Who was that?" His wife Dolly asked as she swept into the kitchen with her bath robe partially open. The belt was tied around her waist but it only served to keep the robe from falling off. Dolly was broad-shouldered and full-breasted. She was long-waisted with well-formed hips that rolled rhythmically as she glided across the floor.

"That was Sherrie," Ted said peering over the top of his cup of coffee. "I've got to go to work," he remarked.

"I know," she said. "Why are you telling me that?"

"If you don't close that robe I ain't gonna make it."

"Ummm," she purred as she straddled his legs, pressed her body against his, and wrapped the robe around them both. He felt her warmth radiating through his cloths.

"You pervert," she whispered softly as she caressed his neck with her lips. "You're really anxious to go?"

They were juniors in high school when they had had their first sexual encounter. Ted was working part-time for her father. Her father was an outfitter and gave tourist trail rides on horseback through the Wind River National Forest. Ted's job was to keep the horse stalls clean; make sure the horses had plenty of water and help Dolly groom them when they returned from a trail ride.

On one such occasion, while Dolly was using a body brush to groom the inside of a male horse's hind legs, its male organ extended itself. Ted was combing the tail of a horse close by and saw what was happening.

"See what you girls do to guys?" Ted commented through a snicker.

"This is no guy," Dolly shot back. "It's a horse."

"Yeah, but he has the same feeling as a guy does, I bet," Ted said. "If a pretty girl was rubbing the inside of my leg I know I'd have a reaction."

Nothing else was said by either of them and they worked through all the horses, gathered up the grooming equipment, and returned them to the tack room. The room was filled with harnesses, bridles, bags of feed, and saddles on stands. After Dolly had put her grooming combs and brushes away, to Ted's surprise, she put her hand on his arm and asked, "Does my touching your arm start any reaction?"

They had fond memories of that day every time they heard "Back in the Saddle Again" by Aerosmith. They married during their senior year and Ted went to work on the ranch full-time after graduation. The tack room became one of their favorite places to meet during the day. Over the years of marriage, they still had not lost their appetite for each other.

While Sherrie was talking to Ted, the light on a second phone line was blinking. Having finished with him she punched the blinking light. "It's Sherrie," she announced.

"Hi, Sherrie, it's Amy with CPI. I'm calling to update you on activities regarding Patricia Anne."

"What's new, Amy?" Sherrie settled back in her chair in anticipation.

"Sister Mary Margaret, from the convent in Dayton, arrived last night and met with hospital administration and doctors this morning. She was told that test had shown a growth on Patricia's brain. Images indicate that it is operable and that it was imperative that it be surgically removed with all haste. Arrangements have been made to airlift Patricia to Salt Lake City. I've advised the court and an order releasing her is being faxed to the hospital. Sister Mary Margaret is planning to accompany Patricia Anne. She intends to get with the department later and make arrangements to take possession of the car and other personal belongings. I'll hand carry copies of all the paperwork to your office once the transport has been made."

"The sheriff and the guys will be glad to get this piece of news. They were all really concerned about her. Hopefully she'll be all right," Sherrie commented.

"According to the neurologist, damage to brain tissue could be substantial, but it won't be known until they get in there," Amy related.

"Okay, Amy. Thanks for the call and we'll see ya soon," Sherrie said.

Ted drove a Bronco II that the department had given him. It was more suitable for the area than a cruiser. Most of his patrolling was on unimproved roads and some were tough to traverse. The old Boutros place was eight miles west of Highway 191 which runs north through the valley. The access road was dirt and Ted noticed that though there were some deep ruts, it appeared to have been well traveled. The fields on either side that had been prime grazing land were now covered with sage brush and tumble weed.

To Ted's surprise, about a hundred yards before reaching the ranch house, an entrance gate had been constructed over the road. Three logs of different heights, encased in concrete at their base, were on each side of the road. The tallest of the three supported a log that stretched over the road, and a board with the name Boutros Ranch burned into it was mounted in the middle. A red pipe cattle gate restricted vehicle entrance to the property and a four-strand barbwire fence ran north and south from the gate as far as he could see. A large padlock secured the gate to the log supports.

"Dispatch, this is SO 12," Ted said into his radio mic.

"SO 12 go ahead," a female voice responded.

"SO 12's 10-20 (location) Boutros Ranch. There has been a gate put across the access road so I'll be 10-6 (busy) walking to the house. Have hand radio."

"10-4 SO 12."

Ted exited his Bronco, climbed over the gate, and walked slowly toward the main house. It was constructed of logs. Ted thought to himself that it was one of those kits that he'd seen advertised. He also noted that there was a metal storage type building with two overhead doors a short distance north of the house. He didn't remember that building being there when the department had the sale.

As he walked the short distance to the house, he pulled his baseball cap forward on his head so the bill would block the sun's reflection off the metal building. Looking down at the road's surface he noticed numerous vehicle tracks on the road that led into the metal building. It was odd that there were no vehicles of any kind in the yard. The sheep pens were still in place on the west side of the house like he remembered them.

There was a porch supported by six varnished logs that matched the exterior of the house and as he stepped up and approached the front door, he noticed a large bay window on the right side of the door and a smaller window on the left side. The smaller window was set a bit higher in the wall than the larger one. Through the bay he could see what appeared to be a dining room table with dirty dishes and empty beer bottles on it. There had been three people at the setting.

Ted knocked on the door and waited. He could hear no movement inside. He knocked again and waited, no sound of movement from inside. He walked toward the metal building and noticed a door that looked like an office door so he tried the knob, it was locked and the upper portion of the door had a glass window that had some type of dark material over it on the inside. As he turned to leave, the sun reflected off something in the sandy soil. Curious, he walked over to it. Partially buried was a metal plate with what appeared to have numbers on it. He picked it up. He recognized it to be a vehicle serial number plate. Again, his curiosity kicked in and he stuck it in the breast pocket of his jacket. He'd check it out later, he thought.

As he walked back toward the gate, he saw dust being kicked up in the distance and he could hear what he thought might be a motorcycle. His Bronco was blocking his view so he just stopped and watched the dust cloud getting closer. He was almost right. It was a four-wheeled all-terrain vehicle. It was painted camouflage and probably used for hunting. The rider was a rather large man with a full beard dressed in coveralls like those that heavy equipment mechanics wear.

"What the hell you do on this property, Deputy?" the large fellow called out after shutting the machine's engine off. "Don't gates with locks mean anything to you?"

They were still some distance apart so rather than yell, Ted began a slow walk toward the gate and took his radio from his belt.

"Dispatch, SO 12," he said into the radio.

"12 this is dispatch."

"10-61 (personnel in area) making contact with individual at entrance to Boutros Ranch on a four wheel ATV."

"10-101 (are you secure), SO 12?"

"10-106 (secure), dispatch."

The man was still seated on the ATV when Ted reached the gate.

"I'm Deputy Harper and I'm here to see the owner of this property," Ted informed him all the while sizing up this individual. He noticed the butt of a revolver sticking out of the left hip pocket of the coveralls. Not unusual for people out here to be carrying a fire arm, he thought.

"You're looking at him, what cha need?"

"Some ID would be helpful, sir, here's mine in case the uniform isn't enough," Ted said as he held up a leather card holder containing a badge and his deputy sheriff's identification card.

"Why you need my ID, you're on my property?"

Ted climbed up and over the gate and maintaining a safe distance continued to converse. "I have no idea who you are, sir, and I'd hate to pass on the information I have to someone who is not entitled to it. Since you're riding that machine off your property and on a county road, if you'll provide me a driver's license and registration, I'll be able to verify who you are."

The bearded fellow unzipped the coveralls, reached inside to the hip pocket of pants he was wearing, and produced a wallet. "I've got a driver's license but I just borrowed this machine to come pick up some tools from my place. I'm working on a ditch witch at a friend's house. This is his machine," he said as he passed the license to Ted. The name on the license was David Cooke, DOB 9/11/56.

"If you'll pardon me a sec while I verify this," Ted said as he moved to his vehicle to use its radio. As he watched through the windshield, David seemed to be antsy and really concerned about what Ted was doing. It took a while because Ted was having dispatch to check the name through the county clerk's office against property records.

"Okay, David, sorry it took so long," Ted said as he handed the license back. "What relation are you to Mr. Bruce Boutros?" he asked.

"I was his nephew, but he's dead and I paid the taxes on the property."

"Yeah, before your uncle died, he made a deal with an institution in Colorado that another relative could come live here after he had finished being treated. Here's a copy of the letter that was faxed to me."

David took the letter, read it, and then handed it back to Ted before he spoke.

"Hell, I'm not beholden to that. I don't need no screw ball running around the place. No, he can't come here, hell no."

"But he's family, David!" Ted exclaimed.

"Not to me, he ain't. Let them keep him in Colorado."

"He's here, David," Ted said.

"What? Where?" David asked.

"He's in Rock Springs."

"Well, you let him stay in Rock Springs, he ain't coming out here, you hear?"

David got off the ATV, unlocked the gate, opened it enough to get the machine through, relocked it, and without another word sped down the road to the metal building and Ted watched as David went inside, opened one of the overhead doors, drive the ATV inside, and the door closed.

CHAPTER

The county commissioner that Craig had the best relationship with was Raul Sosa. He was hardheaded, opinionated, and a Republican, but they had been able to work together on lots of projects. In the past, whenever the jail situation was brought up in meetings, there were always things of higher priorities that available monies had to be used for. This time Craig felt that he had done his homework, but he was going to need help convincing the other four commissioners.

It was just a short walk to where the commissioners had their offices in the courthouse and Craig figured it would be to his advantage to just walk in on Raul without giving him any prior notice. That way he wouldn't have time to think of reasons why something can't be done. He was in luck. Raul was in his office, the door was closed and he was on the phone so Craig waited. He stood where Raul could see him through the glass in the door. Raul's conversation must have been personal because as soon as he saw Craig, he obviously cut the call short and hung up the phone. He motioned to Craig to come in.

"Hey, Craig. What brings you over on this side of the hill?" Raul stood and stuck out his hand which Craig shook enthusiastically.

"Hi ya, Raul," Craig said. "Didn't mean to interrupt your phone call."

"Not a problem, in fact you were a part of the conversation."

"Oh yeah!" Craig exclaimed, somewhat surprised.

"Yeah, that was a buddy of mine in Carbon County, he's one of the commissioners over there. He was asking how you were making out with the ACLU. I was telling him that I knew there was going to be a hearing soon but otherwise, I didn't know. Now that you're here, maybe you can fill me in."

Craig put his hands together as if in prayer and cast his eyes toward the ceiling.

"What's that for"? Raul asked.

"Just thanking the almighty for running interference for me," Craig said as Raul stared in wonderment at the comment. "That's exactly what I'm here for, to talk to you about the ACLU lawsuit. They have sued every county in the state of Wyoming. Your buddy's county, Carbon, just avoided going to trial by signing a "consent decree" in which the county agreed to improve jail conditions or face punishment from the federal court. Carbon County is not alone, Park signed an agreement that said the county would reduce the number of inmates housed in their jail, improve lighting, exercise equipment, and do something about overcrowding. Big Horn had to close their jail for some time because of heating and ventilation conditions. For several years they sent their prisoners to Washakie County jail. It cost them forty dollars a day for adults and ninety dollars a day for juveniles. If we were required to do that, I'd go through my annual budget in no time. By the way, Park County just passed a measure to build a new jail. Sarah and I, on several occasions, have brought to the attention of you, commissioners, that we are skating on thin ice when it comes to our jail. The cells are too small, the plumbing is old and deteriorating, the roof leaks, the jail was designed to hold eighty inmates and we average one hundred twenty on any given day, too many prisoners, not enough room. It's a dangerous situation. You only have to look back at the murder of Watson by Brown to see what I'm saying."

Brown was the murderer that escaped from jail after killing his cellmate and eventually being killed by Craig.

"So, what are you suggesting we do, Craig?" Raul asked with genuine interest.

"Thought you'd never ask," Craig said as he scooted forward in his chair. "With the success that the ACLU has had in having jails shutdown or forcing counties to commit to new facilities or reduce the number of inmates they can house, if we go to court, they'll probably shut us down. We cannot afford that to happen." Craig paused while he took some notes out of his jacket pocket.

"Last year, the state of Wyoming shared close to twenty million dollars of oil and gas revenues with Sweetwater County. According to the treasurer's office, you commissioners have only committed or encumbered three million dollars of that. Since I believe you are highly respected by the rest of the members on the commission, I'm suggesting that you have a friendly talk with the others, advise them of what's happening in the rest of the state, what is almost sure to happen in Sweetwater County, and have them put a proposal on the table at the next commissioners meeting to commit twelve million dollars to be used to construct a new county detention center. That will stop the ACLU dead in their tracks and we won't lose control of the situation. Sarah has managed to get a postponement of the hearing until after the commissioners meeting. We really need to do this, Raul," Craig said as he concluded his remarks.

Raul had started flipping pages in a day timer on his desk while Craig was talking. He traced some notes with his finger and cleared his throat. "Selling this is going to be no easier this time than it's been in the past," Raul began. "Each commissioner has some pet projects that he wants to use that money for. There's parks in Green River, street paving in Superior, replacement of water and sewage lines in Rock Springs . . ."

"Raul," Craig interrupted. "Haven't you been listening to me? If we don't make some commitment to improve the jail, the courts are going to make us house our prisoners in one of the counties that have. Do you realize what that's going to cost Sweetwater County? At the rate of forty dollars a day, with an average of a hundred and twenty inmates at any given time, if my arithmetic is right, you're looking at just short of five thousand dollars a day." Craig paused while he took a pen out his shirt pocket, then he continued. "Got a piece of paper?" He asked.

Raul reached in the center drawer of his desk. "How about a calculator, will that help?"

"You bet," Craig replied. "Now multiply five thousand times seven and then multiply your answer by fifty-two."

"That comes out to $1,820,000," Raul said after punching in the numbers.

"I'd really hate to have to justify wasting that kind of money each year to the voters, knowing that you're eventually going to have to build a new jail anyway, and remember, we still haven't cranked in transportation costs to and from some other jail and back and forth to the courts."

Raul sat back in his chair and looked at the numbers on the calculator for a long moment and Craig watched with creased brow.

"We're scheduled to have a working session day after tomorrow," Raul said. "That's where board of commissioners decides what the priorities for the rest of the year will be. It's not open to the public but we'll be brainstorming with some department heads. Can you get a letter requesting to be on the agenda to the clerk's office before that meeting? In the meantime, I'll do a little lobbying and see if I can generate some interest."

Craig reached into the inside pocket of his jacket and took out an envelope. It was addressed to the Sweetwater County board of commissioners. "I'll drop it off with your clerk as I go out," Craig said with a smile.

Arriving back at his office, Craig was somewhat surprised to find Sherrie Munson and Steve Lolly waiting for him. He could tell from the expressions on their faces that neither were the bearers of good news. Taking a seat in his chair at his desk, he addressed them both. "Which one of you wants to be first to ruin the rest of my day?"

Steve spoke first. "There's good news and bad news," Steve started.

"Can't you ever just deliver good news instead of a dash of both?" Craig smiled as he sat back in his chair.

"Sorry, couldn't pass it up. Nature of the job, boss, but we're really here about the same things. First, Sister Patricia Anne is on her way to

Salt Lake for brain surgery. Wyoming Catholic Dieses is footing the bill. Depending on how you look at it, that's the good news. Second, we've run into a snag regarding Boutros. I'll let Sherrie explain."

"Be gentle, Sherrie," Craig appealed.

"Deputy Harper made contact with the current owner of the main compound at the Boutros place. He's a nephew of old man Boutros, named David Cooke. He has flat refused to honor the agreement that the old man had regarding Kenneth."

"You're telling me that this Cooke person won't allow Kenneth to come stay at the ranch? Is that what you're telling me?" There was frustration in Craig's voice.

"That's what we're telling you, boss," Steve confirmed.

Craig sat for several moments without speaking, just sitting with his hands down on his desk, looking first at Sherrie and then at Steve. There was anger in his eyes and he wasn't trying to hide it. "What's his status at the hospital?" he asked.

"They have him on a different set of meds that seem to help him stay much calmer, he's not as jittery or excitable as he was and according to Amy Dreskel with CPI, he says he feels better now than he has for a long time. The hospital has released him. He's no longer a danger to himself or others so we're going to have to do the same," Sherrie replied.

"I'm not putting that man back on the street with no means of sustaining himself and no place to go. I'm just not gonna do it," Craig was emphatic.

"But, boss, we can't legally continue holding him in lockup," Steve said.

"Who's gonna complain, him?" Craig asked. "We'll hang on to him a couple of days if we have to. In the meantime, here's what I want you to do, have one of the admin clerks contact every nonprofit church organizations, landscaping outfits, and construction people, in that order, see if anyone's looking for hands; if any one says yes, tell them to get ahold of me. In the meantime, I'm going up and visit with Kenneth, any questions?" Both Steve and Sherrie shook their heads indicating that there were no questions. They both knew when it was best to just do as they were told. Craig pulled his hat tight on his head and headed down the hall toward the parking lot and his car.

As Craig walked down the hall toward the lockup rooms, he could see both Fred and Amy Dreskel standing at the table that security officers use. Neither of them saw him coming until he spoke. "To what do I owe the honor of seeing two of my favorite people on the job at the same time?" As they both turned at the sound of his voice, Craig reached out with both arms to embrace Amy. "Hi ya, doll," he said with a big grin on his face. He and Amy had always had a mutual liking for each other.

"Sheriff!" Amy exclaimed as she snuggled in his arms and they gave each other a big squeeze. "It is certainly a surprise to see you here. Are we in trouble?" she asked. Craig clasped hands with Fred and put an arm around his shoulder.

"We do have a situation that we hadn't counted on but it has to do with Kenneth," he said, nodding his head toward the door to the lockup room. "How's he doing?"

"I've been visiting with him," Fred replied. "He's really had a rough time of it. I'm really glad that there is some place for him to go so that he can have a chance to get his life together."

"That's why I'm here," said Craig. "We no longer have a place for him to go. If we release him from here, he's back on the street."

"Uh-uh," Fred said, sort of in a whisper. "He's expecting to be released today and we were finishing up his paperwork. What now?"

"Darn it," Amy whispered. "He was really looking forward to going out to the ranch in Farson. He told me that he was excited about having a place to call home again. What happened?"

"The current owner has declined to honor the agreement that Bruce Boutros made some months ago prior to his passing. I need to find a way to keep him from slipping back, and to keep us from participating in this practice of just shipping people from one jurisdiction to another. I need to visit with him and let him know what's happening."

Fred moved to the outer door of the lockup room where Kenneth was and braced the door open. Amy unlocked the inner door and braced it with her foot, letting Craig into the room.

Kenneth was lying on the bed that had been placed in the room once it was determined that he was no longer a danger to himself or others. He was still dressed in a hospital gown and socks that patients were given to wear. He sat up when Craig entered the room.

"Hi ya, Kenneth," Craig said as he approached the bed and stuck out his hand to shake Kenneth's. "I'm Craig Spence, sheriff of Sweetwater County and have kinda been your host for the last few days."

"Hey, Sheriff," Kenneth said with a slight smile on his face. "The service has been great but the facilities could use an upgrade."

Craig took off his hat and sat on the bed next to Kenneth. "We do our best to give our customers what they pay for," Craig retorted and they both had a light chuckle. "Glad to see you in good spirits because I'm the bearer of some not so good news." There was no change of expression on Kenneth's face. He just looked Craig straight in the eye and waited. Craig continued, "What do you know of the person that currently owns the Boutros ranch?"

"The only person I know is Uncle Bruce. I haven't seen him since I was real young, maybe ten years old or so. My dad brought me up one summer to visit. It wasn't long after that we lost my dad."

"What happened to him?" Craig inquired.

Kenneth looked out into space for a moment or two and then lowering his head to look at his hands clasped tightly together, he spoke softly. "Don't know if I ever knew. Just remember that at some point he wasn't around anymore. It's been so far back and with everything that's happened over the years, I don't know what's real and what's not," Kenneth said as he ran his hand over a deep indent in his upper forehead.

Craig placed a hand on Kenneth's knee and watched his face for any reaction as he spoke. "Your Uncle Bruce passed away a couple of months back and most of the ranch was put up for sale because of back taxes. A person that says he's a nephew ended up with it. He has refused to honor the agreement your uncle made with the treatment center in Colorado."

Kenneth gave a deep sigh and turned his head away from Craig, and just looked off at the wall for a long time. Craig just waited and watched to see what the reaction was going to be.

"Boy, this is some good stuff the doc gave me," Kenneth said. "Any other time I'd be ricocheting off the walls by now. Damn, damn, damn. Just can't get a break in this world."

"Tell me," Craig started. "You were in Vietnam and you were wounded there, why aren't you being cared for by the VA?"

Kenneth lay back on the bed on his side, his knees drawn tight against his midsection and his eyes fixed on the ceiling. "I wasn't in the military," he began. "I worked for a contractor that was a subcontractor to a large defense contractor. Don't ask me how come I remember this and can't remember a lot of other stuff. I recall coming to in a hospital. I have no idea where it was but everybody had slanted eyes and I thought I'm captured, and I went out again, don't know for how long, but the next time I was conscious, I was in the Philippines. That's where all the reconstructive surgeries took place. I had no idea what had happened to me. Stayed in the Philippines a couple of years, lots of rehab and counseling, slowly began to put some things back together. The one thing I've always remembered through it all is lying in the grass, not able to move and bullets, lots of bullets, tearing up the jungle around me." Kenneth paused for a moment and Craig used the opportunity to direct the conversation.

"How'd you get back to the States?" Craig asked.

"One day, a woman from the American consulate shows up, she's got a stack of traveler's checks worth five thousand dollars. The outfit I'd worked for had left what I had coming with the consulate. When the war in Nam was over, the contractor went out of business, she told me. You see, there is no official record with the government that I was ever in Nam. She had me sign five hundred dollars worth of the checks and she went someplace and got cash. She also gave me an airline ticket to Los Angeles, California."

"And the money," Craig inquired, "what happened to all the money you got?"

"A couple of years living out of motels, gotten in trouble and paying fines, all going out and nothing coming in, five thousand dollars don't last long."

The conversation was interrupted by Fred entering the room and beckoning to Craig to come out in the hall.

"What's up?" Craig asked as he left the room.

"Phone call," Fred replied. "Thought you might want to take it rather than call him back. It's the manager of the hardware store here in Rock Springs."

"Spence here," Craig said into the phone.

"Sheriff, this is Carl Tuber, I run the hardware in town," A raspy voice responded.

"Hi ya, Mr. Tuber. What can I do for you?"

"I have a niece that works as a clerk in your office in Green River and she tells me that we may be able to help each other. The young man that's been a helper in my stockroom is leaving for the army next week and I'm going to have to replace him. Think the lad you're working with would be interested?"

"Don't know, Mr. Tuber," Craig said, hardly able to contain his excitement over such quick response. "What would he have to be doing?" Craig inquired.

"Unpack boxes, put wheel barrows, bicycles, lawn mowers, and such together; keep things cleaned up around here, maybe run errands now and then," Mr. Tuber answered.

"Before I ask if he'd be interested, you need to know that this fellow is homeless and will need a lot of help getting his life together. He'll need assistance in making healthcare connections so that he can obtain needed medications and probably require some counseling," Craig advised.

"I'm also affiliated with SWWRAP," Mr. Tuber related.

"What's that?" Craig asked.

"It's the South West Wyoming Recovery Access Program. We provide supportive services to low income veterans and their families.

Our motto is Building Lives-Restoring Hope-We Care. By the way, is he a veteran?"

"Yes and no," Craig said. "He was wounded in Vietnam fighting on our side, but if he's interested I'll let you and he figure that out. Should he be interested, can I have him brought by the store so you can visit with him?"

"Please do," Mr. Tuber said. "I'll be available all day."

As he hung up the phone, Craig turned to see Fred and Amy hugging each other. Amy spoke first. "We could only hear your side of the conversation, but it sure sounds like things could be looking up for Kenneth."

"I know Carl Tuber," Fred said. "He's very active with the chamber of commerce and pretty much runs the Travelers Aid initiative for the Episcopal Church here. If anyone can help Kenneth, he's the man."

Craig had Fred close the outer door to the lockup room and he explained to them what Carl Tuber had told him. They discussed the "what if" things didn't work out. What would be the likely impact on Kenneth, how would he react.

"If this falls through, I really don't see any alternatives to helping this fellow," Craig said sorrowfully.

"Well," Amy began, "as things are now, he's going to be released anyway. If he reacts badly, I guess you could always re-detain him for his own good."

"I guess we'll just have to cross that bridge when we get to it," Craig said with a sigh. "Open up and let's see what we get."

Craig and Fred re-entered the room while Amy stood at the door. Kenneth was still lying on the bed looking up at the ceiling.

"You believe in the almighty, Mr.?" Craig asked.

"Sheriff, it's been tough," Kenneth began." That's the only thing that's kept me going all these years. Lots of times I don't understand why things happen to me, but I believe there's something better for me out there and a higher power has been watching over me."

"I think you're right and today he smiled on ya. That phone call was a man who wants to give you a job and help you put some meaning in your life."

Kenneth sat up slowly and Craig saw some expression on his face for the first time.

"Does he know about me?" Kenneth asked.

"Pretty much," Craig answered. "You can fill in the blanks because he wants to meet you."

"What kind of a job has he got, Sheriff? It's been a long time since I worked for anybody." There was a little apprehension in Kenneth's voice.

"It's at a hardware store. Unpacking boxes and putting bicycles, wagons, wheel barrows, and stuff together; keeping the place clean and such." Craig explained.

"I can do that," Kenneth affirmed.

"What do we have to do to clear him out of here?" Craig asked Fred.

"Nothing," Fred said. "We have his release papers and thirty days worth of meds. Just need to give him his cloths so he can get dressed and he's good to go."

"When he's ready, can you get him down to the store to meet with Carl?"

"You bet," Fred said as he took a brown paper bag with Kenneth's cloths from Amy.

"Kenneth," Craig said as he put his arms around his shoulders. "Good luck, I hope this will be a new start."

"Sheriff, God bless you. This is the first time ever that I've been released from a place and wasn't all doped up and given a bus ticket and sent off to nowhere," Kenneth said with tears in his eyes as he embraced Craig with a genuine show of appreciation.

Craig put his hat on, a little further forward on his head than usual, and he hurried from the room. As he passed Amy at the lockup room door, she extended her arm, with a tissue in her hand. Craig took it and she watched him stride down the hall, shoulders squared and at marching cadence. She saw him dab his eyes before disappearing around the corner heading to the hospital exit.

CHAPTER

Steve Lolly had spent the better part of his morning out at the Sweetwater Coal Mine. His intent was to visit with a mister Tom Hastard who was the mine's safety officer and was also in charge of security measures and the contracted security force. Steve was aware that Fred and Amy Dreskel's firm was contracted by the mine to provide physical security but this was the first time he had seen them in action. He was required to sign the visitors book—time of entry, his name, the name of the organization he represented and whom he wished to visit. The security officer viewed the information and asked, "Are you armed sir?"

"Yes," Steve replied.

The security officer pointed to a sign on the wall which read, "No firearms past this point." Somewhat surprised, Steve pointed to the column in the visitor's book where he had indicated that he was with the Sweetwater sheriff's department.

"Yes, sir," the security officer said. "That's why I asked if you were armed. No firearms are allowed on the premises. We have a lock box under the counter where we secure your weapon until you exit the property."

Reluctantly, Steve reached inside his jacket, removed his snub nosed chief special from its shoulder holster, removed the bullets and passed it to the officer, who placed it in the lock box and handed Steve the key.

"When you leave, sir, return the key and the officer on duty will return your piece." With that the security officer made a phone call and advised Tom Hastard that a Mr. Steve Lolly from the sheriff's office was at the guardhouse awaiting escort.

While he waited, Steve observed the activity that went on as employees came and went through the guardhouse. Lunch boxes and any packages were inspected for any prohibited items going and coming. Women's purses were inspected. Steve was amused at one female trying to leave, who was upset because she was asked to empty her purse on the counter. After some loud protesting from her and some angry words from others in line behind her, she complied. Apparently, the way things were placed in her purse alerted the officer that something was amiss and sure enough, she confiscated a special tool that had the company's name stamped on it. The officer thanked her for her cooperation and allowed her to leave. "These people are sharp," Steve thought.

Shortly after the purse incident, a short, stocky man wearing a white hard hat entered the guardhouse. He sported a full black beard and wore his hair in a pony tail that protruded from under the back of the hard hat. As soon as he had closed the door behind him, the guard that had been doing the inspections addressed him. "Mr. Hastard," she said, "since you're here, I'll just give this to you now rather than at the end of the shift." She passed him a form she had filled out along with the tool that she had confiscated.

He took a moment to review the form and then spoke. "I can't believe she would jeopardize a good job for this," referring to the tool. He then turned to Steve. "Are you Mr. Lolly?" he asked.

"I am, Mr. Hastard. We spoke on the phone earlier," Steve replied.

"Yes, my office is just across the way, please come with me," Hastard said as he led Steve out of the guardhouse.

The safety office was in one end of a large portable construction trailer which also served as a classroom where Hastard was able to conduct mandatory safety, emergency medical and fire suppression training. On a conference table, there were several small stacks of papers and Hastard invited Steve to have a seat at the table.

"What you see here are copies of time cards that show which

employees were on shift at the motor pool during the week that the bushing disappeared," Hastard explained. "When employees start their shift, they punch in at the time clock in their departments and when they go off duty, they punch out. At the end of the shift the shift supervisor verifies that the data on the card is correct by initialing it." Hastard paused a moment giving Steve an opportunity to view the copies of the time cards and understand what information could be derived from them, and then he continued. "I'm not supposed to have access to employee time cards so I have no idea how you came to have these copies," he said, pausing again until Steve nodded, indicating that he understood.

"There are also copies of task orders for that same period. When there is a need for a special vehicle or some piece of heavy equipment at some location on the mine property, the requesting party submits a task order to the equipment pool. The order provides the type of equipment required; at what location the equipment is needed, the time it is required to be there, details of the task to be performed, and the name of the person making the request." Again, Hastard paused, this time he picked up the copy of the task order form and directed Steve's attention to some additional columns.

"The motor pool dispatcher assigns the task order to an operator and he places the operator's name in the appropriate column on the order. Each piece of equipment has an odometer and before leaving the pool, the operator enters the odometer reading. When the task has been completed, the person that requested the equipment puts in the time the equipment was released and signs his or her name. Notice that military time is used, 0001 through 2400 hours. This is so that there is no confusion as to the time of day. The operator enters the odometer reading again when the equipment is returned, along with the time that the equipment was parked. I've made copies of all the task orders and equipment logs for equipment that could have been used."

"Did you see any red flags while you were putting this together?" Steve asked.

"Can't say that I did, nothing really jumped out at me," Hastard replied.

"One other question," Steve said. "How many people know about this investigation?"

"You can't keep anything secret in a place like this. It's pretty much common knowledge."

"Mr. Hastard, I'm going to ask a big favor of you. These papers may become part of the evidence package. Please date and initial the back of each sheet for me and I'll take them back to the office and have our chief of detectives do an analysis. If we find anything or have questions, we'll give you a call."

"I won't initial the copies of the time cards but I will the others," Hastard said as he began to comply. "Should you call, use the main number for the mine. Should I not be in the office, the switch board will get me on the radio and I'll return your call. Here's my card with my office number as well as the main number."

"Sure, appreciate your help on this," Steve said as he took a large envelope containing the papers from Hastard. "I'll see to it you're kept informed."

It was close to noon when Steve arrived back at the sheriff's office and he found Kevin at his desk, his foot in a chair to keep that bad leg elevated and munching on cashews. Kevin always kept a can in the lower drawer of his desk. Steve placed the envelope containing the copies of logs time cards and task orders on the desk and explained the operating procedures at the mine and the information that would be reflected on the copies. "A close examination of these copies should tell us what employees were on duty the night that bushing left the mine; what piece of equipment was used to put it on the truck, who operated it, and who likely authorized that truck to leave the site," Steve explained.

"Well, I'm not going anywhere so I'll get on it," Kevin said.

"If you run into anything, I'll be in my office putting all this information in report form," Steve advised.

Ted Harper decided to take a break from his patrolling and serving of papers so he stopped at the Farson General Store. It was a great place to visit with the locals and visitors to the area. The store was noted for the large ice cream cones that they served. People would come for miles around, especially on weekends, just to get an ice cream cone.

"Dispatch, this is SO-12," he said into the radio mic as he pulled up to the store.

"Go ahead 12," came the reply.

"12 is 10-6 (busy unless urgent) Farson Store."

"10-4 (okay) SO 12 and by the way when you have a chance give me a 10-21 (call by phone)."

"10-4 dispatch," he responded.

Ted ordered a cone with chocolate swirl from the clerk and begged her to only put half of what is usually put on the cone. He took a few moments to visit with several of the customers and then moved to the restrooms where there was a pay phone on the wall. Putting two quarters in the slot got him a dial tone and he dialed the number to dispatch.

"Sweetwater County Sheriff's Office–Communications Center. How may I help you?"

"This is Ted, what's up?"

"I ran that vehicle ID plate you wanted us to check on," the dispatcher said. "It belonged to a 1979 Ford 250, four-wheel drive, registered to a Don Briscoe out of Pinedale, Wyoming. I don't know what you're into, but that vehicle was reported stolen a month ago."

Ted had just taken a large bite of ice cream from his cone and hearing what dispatch had said, he was just holding it in his month. He got brain freeze and wrapped his forehead in his arm to try and warm it up. When he was more comfortable, he visualized all the tire tracks that he had seen at the Boutros place. He also remembered how antsy Cooke appeared to be when he was checking him out. Is it possible that there is a chop operation going on there?" he asked himself.

"SO 12 are you still there?"

"Yeah, I'm sorry. Just froze my head with some ice cream. Is the sheriff in?" he asked.

"I'll connect you to his line, stand by," she responded and Ted continued licking the ice cream that had started to melt and run down the side of his cone.

"Hi ya, Ted. How's the misses?" Craig was on the other end.

"She's okay, Sheriff, thanks for asking," Ted responded. "I think I may have stumbled onto something and I want your advice on how to proceed," Ted advised.

"Whatcha got?" Craig inquired and Ted filled him in on the situation. "Sounds like you might be on to something. I must admit that I don't have any experience with the type of activity you may be dealing with, so here's my suggestion, get a hold of the Wyoming division of criminal investigation, find out all you can about chop shop operations and what they may be willing to share about operations in the state. Come on down to the meeting tomorrow morning and we'll put our heads together."

"I'll see you in the morning, Sheriff. Thanks."

"Okay, give my best to your wife. See you tomorrow." And the connection was broken.

Craig hadn't gone home for lunch and he wanted to check in and see how Martha was doing. He dialed the house number and got a busy signal. He waited a few moments and tried again, again a busy signal. He surmised that his daughter, Katie, must be on the phone so he decided to visit with Steve and Kevin about the Sweetwater mine case, then he'd call it a day and go home.

Craig found the two of them in Steve's office; Kevin, leaning on a crutch, was looking over Steve's shoulder as they mulled over a desk full of papers.

"You fellows too busy to visit for a minute?" Craig asked.

"Hey, boss," Steve said as he stood respectfully. "Not at all. We're trying to determine who might be involved in the Sweetwater mine situation."

"How's it coming?" Craig inquired.

"Tom Hastard, the safety officer at the mine, gave me some copies of time cards, task orders, and equipment operator logs for that week that the bushing went out," Steve began. "Kevin's been going through them and I'll let him tell you what he's found."

There were two chairs in front of Steve's desk and Craig settled into one of them, pushed his cowboy hat back on his head, and gave Kevin his attention.

"We mentioned before that according to union rules out there, no one performs tasks that someone else has been hired to do," Kevin began. "Since that bushing had to be loaded using a piece of heavy equipment, I began looking to see who the operator on duty that night was. A guy by the name of Junior Hastings was on shift that night. The copy of his time card shows that he clocked in at 2202, February 8. Employees generally clock in for the night shift between 2200 and 2215 and that's the night the bushing went out on the truck owned by Jackman Trucking, out of Salt Lake, according to the security log at the power plant. A task order showed that Hastings was to have a D9 Cat, which is like a bulldozer, at pit #5 at 0210 hours. I checked with the security company and apparently, the mine has seven open pits that they are taking coal out of," Kevin explained. He then placed two sheets of paper on the desk in front of Craig and continued, "The sheet on the left is the task order given to Hastings on the eighth of February. It shows that he returned the CAT to the pool at 0342. The sheet on the right is a copy of the security log from the power plant that I picked up when we first got the case. It shows that the truck exited the plant at 0307 hours, little over thirty minutes before Hastings got back from the pit. Here's why that information is important," Kevin paused while he retrieved another sheet of paper and placed it in front of Craig. "This is the operators log for a rough terrain forklift. It shows that it was used for fifteen minutes on the eighth. According to the log, it was used from 0255 to 0310. The first problem is that the name of the operator entered on the log is Junior Hastings, who wasn't back yet. The second problem is that there is no task order for that piece of equipment, and the third is that Hastings's signature is not consistent with his signature on other logs and task orders."

"What's different?" Craig asked.

"Junior always signs his whole name, Junior Hastings. The signature entered on the log of the forklift on the eighth of February is J Hastings," Kevin said as he pointed out the two signatures to Craig on separate equipment logs. "Whoever signed the log didn't have access to the other logs, so they couldn't imitate Junior's signature."

"Uh-huh," Craig said. "Appears that there may be a rat in the wood pile. Who would have had access to the equipment?"

"As far as I can tell, boss, it would be the equipment pool supervisor," Steve volunteered.

"Do we know who the supervisor was?" Craig asked.

"The name on the task order that sent Hastings to the pit is Tony Pasturie," Kevin responded.

Craig stood up, adjusted his hat, and looked at all the papers strewn across Steve's desk. "It'll be interesting to hear what Pasturie has to say. Stay with it, boys," Craig said as he moved toward the office door. "I'm headed to the house if you need me. Haven't checked on Martha all day. See ya." And he walked out of the room.

Steve began to organize the copies on the desk. He put all the time card copies in one stack, the task orders and equipment logs in their separate stacks. As he handled the equipment logs, several slipped from his hands and fell to the floor. As he stooped to pick them up, he sank to one knee and yelled. "Holy crap!" he exclaimed.

"What's wrong?" Kevin inquired.

"Come, look at this," Steve said, frozen in the same position. One of the sheets had landed facedown on the floor, exposing the date and initials on the back—T H 3/2/82.

"Look at that H," Steve said as he searched the pile for the forklift log. Finding it, he laid it on the floor and put the upside-down sheet next to the signature.

"I'll be damned," Kevin said.

Steve sat on the floor and leaned back against the desk. Neither of them spoke. They just stared at the papers on the floor for a long time. Kevin was the first to speak. "We need to put him at the mine in the early morning of February eighth."

"Yeah," Steve said, almost woefully. "That's going to be a toughie." He picked up the papers from the floor and sat at his desk. "This guy has a pretty cushy job out there and I'm betting his salary is in the six-figure range. Why would he be involved in the theft of this bushing?" Steve was thinking out loud.

"Let's get Fred or Amy Dreskel in here," Kevin suggested. "If anyone would know this guy, they would. He actually administers their security contract so I'll bet they visit quite a bit."

"Won't we be putting them in the middle? They work for this guy," Steve cautioned.

"Yep," Kevin responded. "They work for us too. You got a better idea?"

Steve shook his head indicating that he didn't. He took his handset radio from his belt and spoke into it, "Dispatch, SO-2."

The response was immediate. "SO-2, this is Dispatch."

"Dispatch, get to CPI and see when it would be convenient to meet. Their place or ours, don't matter."

"10-4, SO-2, stand by."

Steve began putting the sheets of paper into an envelope while he waited. Once he had it filled, Kevin provided him an evidence tag which he filled out and adhered to the packet.

"SO-2, Dispatch."

"Go ahead, Dispatch," Steve responded.

"Amy Dreskel is the only one available," the dispatcher was saying. "Fred is in Montana handling a personnel problem at one of their sites. She is available at their offices all day today and tomorrow."

"Advise her that I'll stop in around 9:00 AM tomorrow," Steve said and the dispatcher acknowledged.

The weather was half decent, Craig thought, as he crossed the street to the residence that the county provided the sheriff. It was one of those rare occasions when the wind wasn't blowing forty miles an hour. When he reached the top of the stairs that led to the front door, he stopped. From the front of his house he could look over downtown and see the

Green River as it meandered through the outskirts and into the canyon as it headed south to Utah. He loved that view.

The front door opened into a grand living room well furnished with Western-styled furniture. When he stepped inside, Craig immediately noticed that the phone next to the recliner he generally sat in was off the hook. There were four phones in the house, the one in the living room, an extension in the kitchen, the master bedroom, and upstairs in Katie's living area. Craig stood, listening for any sound of activity. All he heard was the faint sound of the busy signal coming from the phone. He quietly moved through the house and as he approached the kitchen, he heard music. Martha always kept a small radio in the kitchen that she listened to when she was busy there. As he entered the kitchen, there was Katie stirring something in a steaming pot on the stove. Just as she reached for a measuring cup filled with water, Craig spoke. "Hi ya, doll?" he said.

Startled, Katie yelled, "Hot damned son of a bitch!" The measuring cup flew out of her hand as she grasped her chest, the water soaking the front of her shirt and jeans. "Dad!" she exclaimed. "You scared the piss out of me."

"Hell, I'm sorry, baby. I didn't mean to scare you," Craig apologized as he hurriedly picked up the measuring cup from the floor and took Katie in his arms. "Forgive me?"

"I need you to put two cups of water in the pot before that stew burns. I've got to sit down," she said, trying to catch her breath.

"What's with the phone off the hook in the living room?" he asked as he drew water from the faucet over the sink.

"Mom's trying to rest. I took that one off the hook so we wouldn't have to listen to the dial tone."

"How is she doing?" Craig inquired.

"That radiation is kicking her butt," Katie responded. "The radiologist said that she would experience increased fatigue over the next three weeks or so, then it would probably not get any worse but she'll feel fatigued for the duration of the treatment. She'll also lose her appetite."

"Are you two talking about me behind my back?" Martha was standing in the kitchen doorway, holding her robe tight around her neck.

She looked so tired, Craig thought. He walked over to her, took her by the arm, and led her to a chair at the kitchen table. Once she was seated, he leaned over and kissed her forehead.

"Can I get you anything, doll?" he asked with obvious concern in his voice.

"No, just sit with me a minute and hold my hand," she said, and Craig pulled up a chair beside her and held her hand and she laid her head on his shoulder.

"What happened to you?" Martha asked Katie.

"My father snuck in and scared the hell out of me. I was holding a thing of water and it ended up all over me."

"Shame on you, Craig," Martha scolded lovingly. "Glad it wasn't hot grease she was holding."

"While you two visit, I'm going to go get out of this wet shirt and I'll put the phone back on the hook on my way up," Katie called out as she moved through the kitchen door into the living room.

When Craig entered the room for the 7:30 morning meeting, the staff was already there. He greeted them enthusiastically. "Hi ya, team! And welcome to the mad house, Ted." He was referring to Ted Harper, the deputy from Farson.

"Thank you, Sheriff. It's nice to talk to someone other than dispatch for a change," Ted quipped.

"Well, I think we've got lots to talk about so let's get started," Craig began. "What's happening in your area, Sherrie?"

"Pretty routine," she started. "We have 119 house quests, seven will be making their first court appearances and three will be going to trial. We have two in emergency detention. One is a female that attacked an officer when he tried to remove her from a bus last night. Apparently, Dora Petri is her name, had been cursing and physically mistreating passengers. The other, also female, is a local teenager from green River, attempted suicide. According to the intake report from Amy at CPI, she had dealt with Dora several years back in Commerce City, Colorado. She says that Dora suffers from dual personalities."

"What's the problem with the teen?" Craig was curious.

"According to the mother who came to the hospital with her, she had been molested by her dad. She signed a complaint and he's one of those making an initial appearance today," Sherrie responded.

"What's the status of the teen, do you know?" Craig continued to inquire.

"She took an unknown number of her mother's hydrocodone and naproxen. Her stomach was pumped and she is now under guard in ICU. They don't want her pulling out the IVs and such, and they're watching to see that she doesn't crash on them."

"You might keep a special watch on the father. News travels fast among inmates and they don't take kindly to molesters and rapist," Craig cautioned. "How's progress with the Brass Ring Kevin?" The question was met with some chuckles from the group.

"After you left us yesterday, Steve and I were messing with the papers and we found what we believe to be a match for that H."

"Ya don't say," Craig said. "How'd you find it?"

"When Steve picked the papers up from Tom Hastard out at the mine, he had him date and initial them on the back. The H in those initials matches the one on the operator's log that Hastings, the heavy equipment operator, supposedly signed."

"Can you put him on the mine property that night?" Craig was somewhat skeptical.

"I'm working on that, boss," Steve spoke up. "I have a meeting with Amy Dreskel at CPI this morning. They have a login process so that they know who's on the property at any given time."

"Can't say that I'd be surprised if someone in a high position was involved in this," Craig said. "What will be more interesting is why. You two working on anything else?"

Both Kevin and Steve shook their heads indicating the negative. Craig took a small notebook from the breast pocket of his shirt, made some notes, and returned the book to the pocket. He always kept notes so that he wouldn't forget to follow-up on stuff. Then he moved to another topic. "I've asked Ted to come to the meeting today because he may have stumbled onto some activity in the county that we are unaware of and frankly, I don't think any of us know too much about. I'll let Ted take it from here."

"When I went out to the Boutros ranch to see about Kenneth staying there, there was no one around at first," Ted began. "While I was checking to see if anyone might be in some of the outbuildings, I noticed what I recognized to be a vehicle VIN plate. Curious, I picked it up and put it in my pocket. As I was returning to my patrol unit, a guy comes up on an ATV and is not too happy that I'm on the property. Oh yeah, there is an elaborate gate that's been built across the road and I'm on one side and he's on the other. After I crawl over the gate and tell him I'm looking for the owner, he identifies himself as the owner. He was reluctant to show me an ID, but he finally did and his name was David Cooke, and he was nervous when I had dispatch checking things out. Sure nuf, he checks out to be the owner. He also tells me that he's a nephew of old man Boutros. When I tell him why I'm there and shows him a copy of the letter from that place in Colorado, he really got belligerent and made it clear that Kenneth could not come to live there. He went through the gate and drove the ATV into a large maintenance type building. That building was locked when I tried to open the door. When I went home for lunch, I called Sherrie on the phone, and told her the story and asked dispatch to check out the VIN. Turns out, it belongs to a pickup that had been reported stolen." Ted paused while he opened an aluminum cruiser mate (a clipboard that has several storage compartments that officers use to keep maps, citation pads, and any written forms that they regularly use). He removed several small groupings of papers, clipped together with paper clips, and he passed one to each member of the staff and to Craig. "Like you suggested, Sheriff, I contacted the WDCI (Wyoming Division of Criminal Investigation). While I was on the phone with them, I found out that they have been trying to get a lead on an auto theft ring that they suspect is operating in the state. They faxed me some information on chop shop operations that may be of use to us and that's what I've passed around. In case any of you need to go out there, I saw where three people had eaten and each had a beer. I don't know if they stay there or if they were visitors. Also, this guy Cooke was packing. I saw the butt of a revolver sticking out of the hip pocket of his coveralls, so be careful."

"When I have a minute, I'm going to familiarize myself with this," Craig said as he thumbed through the pages that Ted had passed out. "Ted, I want you to pick out a spot where we can conduct some surveillance. Steve, when you visit with Amy over at CPI, see if she might be able to spare some people to watch the place. I want to know what comes in and what goes out of that ranch."

*****

Back in his office, Craig notices a message on the spindle—"Call Sarah ASAP"—it said. He thought it unusual that Sarah would be calling him. *Must be important,* he thought, as he dialed her number.

"This is Sarah," she answered.

"Hi ya, Craig here."

"You can chalk up another one for your persuasive personality," she said.

"I'm not with you, doll," Craig responded, somewhat confused.

"You won't have to be at this month's commissioners meeting," she advised.

"How come?" Craig inquired.

"Raul is going to bring up the situation during his turn on the agenda when each commissioner gives their comments and reports. He's going to make a motion that the planning department and the county engineer come up with a preliminary design, a potential location for a detention center and estimated costs, and that the plan be presented to the board at next month's meeting," Sarah explained. "The rest of the commissioners have agreed to support it."

"Good ole Raul," Craig commented. "I'll have to let him know how much I appreciate him carrying the ball for us. I thank you for letting me know the good news."

"You're welcome. See ya." She hung up.

*****

Amy had been at her desk since daybreak, creating schedules for the security teams at Sweetwater Mine, a fertilizer plant south of town, two soda ash mines west of Green River, a Bureau of Mines facility in Salt Lake City, Utah, and the emergency detention lockup at the hospital.

She had spent several hours at the hospital during the night when the PD brought in a lady named Dora Petri.

Amy remembered Dora from a period when she was a patrol officer in Commerce City, Colorado, a few years back. Every so often, Amy would be detailed to transport Dora to the state hospital. A petite little lady, Dora reminded Amy of Mrs. Santa Clause as she was portrayed in children's books. A full head of white curly hair that framed a face with pudgy cheeks, dark eyes under white brows that looked over narrow lenses that rested on the end of her nose. That's where the likeness ended. Dora had command of the most vulgar language and could spew out the vilest rhetoric that Amy had ever heard and on this night, Dora did not hesitate to go into a blistering tirade as she recalled their past associations. As she was being bombarded with obscenities, Amy knew that this would go on until a switch would flip and Dora would turn into a very articulate person, knowledgeable of social and governmental affairs, and very respectful of those around her. The switch didn't flip last night.

Amy was pouring herself another cup of coffee, when her office manager announced the arrival of Steve Lolly from the sheriff's office. She poured a second cup of coffee and called out. "Come on in, Steve, the coffee's hot."

"Hey, Amy," Steve said as he accepted the cup of coffee that Amy held out to him. "How come Fred left you all alone."

"Had an employee that needed firing, and he does that better than me. Every time I fire somebody, we end up being sued." They both chuckled as Amy proceeded to close the office door. "What's on your mind, Steve?"

"We may have made some headway on the Brass Bushing incident," Steve began. "We've always known that it was an inside job but now we've identified some of the players."

"That's great, Steve, mine management will be excited about that," Amy said.

"Maybe not," Steve cautioned.

"Uh-uh," Amy said, cupping her coffee cup in both hands. "That sounds ominous."

"We believe that one of the players is a person that holds a prominent staff position. In fact, we believe Hastard may be up to his ears in this." Steve paused and looked over the rim of his cup to observe Amy's reaction. To his surprise, she just kept sipping her coffee, looking him in the eye over the rim of her cup, which she still held with both hands as if to keep them warm. Steve continued. "We need your help."

For a long moment, Amy didn't speak. She sat her coffee cup down and leaned back in her chair. Tom Hastard was more a friend than the manager of CPI's contract. Many times, he, she, and Fred had visited over drinks and shared much about their private lives. For example, Tom had shared the fact that he and his wife loved to gamble and that they spent many of their weekends at the Wind River Casino in Riverton, Wyoming, or the Bingo Halls in Cheyenne and Casper. *Was there a connection?* she asked herself. *What a predicament,* she thought.

"How can I help, Steve?" Amy finally inquired.

"We need to put Hastard on site after midnight on February 8. Do your people keep any type of logs?"

"Sure," Amy responded. "There are two parking lots. Hourly employees park in one outside the main gate next to the guardhouse and administrators, staff and supervisors park in a lot inside the main gate. All vehicles and persons that go inside the main gate are logged in and out."

"What's the chance that I can get a copy of the logs for February 8?" Steve asked.

"Slim," Amy said almost before Steve finished asking and he sat starring at her, as if he couldn't believe she said that. "I didn't say it was impossible," she continued with a smile, amused by his reaction. "I can't give you any copies without getting permission. Normally, in cases like this, I'd run it by Tom. Under the circumstances, that's not a good idea."

"I don't quite understand," Steve said. "What do you suggest?"

"Those logs belong to the mine, so I'm not going to give them to you. Here's what I will do," Amy became very serious. "Periodically,

I check the logs to make sure that the guards are filling them out properly. If I see that Tom entered the mine after normal work hours on the eighth, I'll let you know. Then you can call the mine CEO and request copies. No sense alerting anybody until we know that what you need is there."

"Won't he want to know why I don't ask Hastard?" Steve asked.

"Yup, I'm sure you can come up with a good reason," Amy said. "I'll go out and check those logs at shift change this afternoon. Is that okay?"

"You bet," Steve responded. "One other question, do you have any idea why he might involve himself in something like this?"

"I have no idea, Steve. I am aware that he spends a lot of his weekends at casinos around the state. Is there a connection? I can't say."

"Thanks, Amy, really appreciate your help. By the way, we have another situation that we could really use your help on."

"What do you have?" Amy inquired.

Steve spent several moments laying out what the sheriff thought might be happening at the Boutros ranch. While he was explaining the situation to her, Amy took notes and took a road map out of file box on her desk and laid it out.

"I'm not familiar with the ranch. Can you point out its general location?" she asked.

Leaning over the desk, Steve traced his finger along Highway 28 to a point west of Farson, took his pen from his breast pocket and put an X to mark the location.

"When do you anticipate starting the surveillance?" Amy asked.

"As soon as you can put it together, I guess," Steve replied.

"I'll run this by Fred when he gets back. Shouldn't be more than a couple of days, if you're not in a hurry," she said. "We've got a couple of people that are avid hunters and have all types of spotting scopes and range finders that'll come in handy."

"I think that's okay," Steve said. "We don't have a plan yet and we'll need to stage the area."

"It looks like it's pretty flat out there, not much concealment," Amy observed.

"When Fred gets back, we'll get him together with Ted Harper, he's the deputy in Farson, and get a plan put together," Steve said. "Gotta go. Give me a call when you've checked those logs, and thanks again, Amy." Steve got up and headed for the door with Amy in escort. "I'm sorry if we've put you in a bad spot."

"No, you're not," Amy scolded. "Give my best to the sheriff."

After Steve had gone, Amy began thinking about Dora. She recalled that Dora had, at one time, taught social science classes at a private school somewhere West of Denver, Colorado. At some point, Doreen, her second personality, showed up and she had been in and out of institutions ever since.

Amy decided to put in a call to an old friend at the state hospital in Pueblo, Colorado. Toby White had been a patrolman on Commerce City PD like herself. He retired and went to work as a security guard at the hospital. Hopefully he was still there.

After being transferred to several different phones, she was finally connected to Toby who was now the day shift commander and a lieutenant on the guard force.

"Lt. White," he answered the phone.

"Boy, you've done well for yourself," Amy commented.

"Are you sure you have the right number?" Toby asked.

"Yeah, Toby, this is Amy, Amy Crawford," she said, thinking that he would recognize her maiden name.

"Amy Crawford!" he exclaimed. "Hell, talk about a blast from the past."

Amy and Toby conversed for several moments, reconnecting and bringing each other up-to-date on family and both their marriages; Amy informed him of the success she was having as co-owner of the security company and they both enjoyed the visit.

"Toby," she finally said, "I've just run into an old acquaintance of ours."

"That so, who's that?"

"Dora Petri," she said.

"Are you kidding, she walked away from here over a year ago," he said. "She was committed by the courts and there's an active warrant out on her."

"Well, she's in Rock Springs, Wyoming, and we have her in emergency detention. She got thrown off a bus for harassing the passengers."

"Doreen is alive and well huh? When she was here, Doreen was in control for longer periods of time and she was becoming more violent," Toby advised.

"You guys want her back?" Amy crossed here fingers as she waited for him to answer.

"You bet," Toby responded. "I'll start making arrangements to have you guys ship her down."

"If you would, I'd really appreciate it," Amy replied. "I'm looking forward to hearing from you."

*****

Craig spent all morning browsing through copies of reports that his records clerk had left for him. There were instances of domestic violence, vandalism, public intoxication, and shoplifting, possession of controlled substance, barking dogs, and DWIs, routine stuff. He decided to take this opportunity and familiarize himself with the stuff Ted had passed out. The first page was the U.S. Code which described and defined what a chop shop was.

"In general, any person who knowingly owns, operates, maintains, or controls a chop shop or conducts operations in a chop shop, shall be punished by a fine or imprisoned for not more than fifteen years or both. Under the code, the term "chop shop" means any building, lot, or other structure or premise where one or more persons engage in receiving, concealing, destroying, disassembling, dismantling, reassembling, or storing any passenger motor vehicle or passenger vehicle which has been unlawfully obtained in order to alter, counterfeit, deface, destroy, disguise, falsify, remove the identity, including the vehicle identification number, for the purpose of selling or otherwise disposing of the vehicle or its parts."

The second page described how a chop shop operates and the agent supplying the information was quick to indicate that rarely do you see operations like the ones you see in the movies—huge buildings with rows of expensive cars and teams of mechanics. Most shops operate out of small houses, residential garages, or nondescript commercial spaces. The goal of the operators is quick turnaround. Cars are taken in, taken apart, and moved out within a few short hours. Small individual shops are generally part of a larger network of thieves and illicit salvage yards. The thieves steal vehicles according to a list provided by the chop shop or the salvage yard source. The Thieves also take orders from crooked used car dealers and drug runners. They run stolen vehicles through the chop shop where the identification numbers and such are removed, may even be repainted prior to delivery.

On the third page, the agent wrote, "Because of an uptick in auto thefts this year, the attorney general had asked that we get involved and provide local enforcement with whatever assistance we could. We developed an informant that's associated at ABC Towing in Kemmerer, Wyoming. They do repos and operate all over the state. Mysteriously, we lost contact with the snitch about a week ago. He also hunts coyotes and drives a 1980 Dodge truck painted camouflage. He always has an ATV on the truck. Would appreciate you guys keeping an eye out and if you spot him, let us know."

Craig's concentration was interrupted by the phone on his desk ringing. A light was flashing but he pushed the button marked SB for switch board.

"Who you got?" Craig asked.

"It's Sister Mary Margaret, she asked to speak with you," was the reply. Craig immediately came to his feet. He had always been told to stand when being spoken to by a nun or a priest. He pushed the flashing button.

"This is Sheriff Spence," he said into the phone.

"Good day, Sheriff, this is Sister Mary Margaret from the Sisters of the Sacred Heart in Dayton."

"It's great hearing from you, Sister. Sorry I missed you when you were here," Craig addressed her respectfully and in his most charming tone of voice. "How is Sister Patricia Anne?"

"That's why I wished to speak with you. I was making arrangements for her car to be brought to Dayton and I wanted to take this opportunity to thank you on behalf of the Dieses for the part your people played in the care of Sister Patricia Anne. I'm happy to tell you that through the deft hands of the surgeons, throughout a twelve-hour ordeal, the heavenly father has seen fit to allow the sister to remain with us. We do know that she will need speech therapy and probably physical therapy to help her regain the ability to walk without assistance. Other than that, we'll just have to wait and pray."

"Please, Sister, when you can, let her know that she'll be in our prayers," Craig said.

"And you in ours, Sheriff Spence, Goodbye." She was gone.

Craig was still holding the phone to his ear thinking, *Boy I'll bet she runs a tight ship,* when Steve came in.

"Busy, boss?" As usual, Steve didn't wait for an answer. "Just got a call from Amy Dreskel. Tom Hastard entered the mine property at midnight on February 8 and checked out at 0410. She checked and he never logged back in that day so she suspects that he was off. I need a copy of that log sheet but she won't give it to me. She suggests that you call the CEO and request a copy. She says that if you just tell him you're trying to tie up some lose ends regarding the investigation, he won't ask too many questions."

"Just curious," Craig started. "Is it unusual for staff to be showing up at that time of night?"

"No, boss," Steve responded. "According to Amy, people having to do with safety, security, and mine production schedules frequently show up at all hours." Steve passed a sticky note to Craig. "Here's the CEO's name, Jeb McKenney, and direct phone number."

"Okay, I'll give him a jingle and get back with you."

CHAPTER 7

It's was always a stressful endeavor when a member of the staff had to be cut loose. Fred treated all the employees like family, and when he had to terminate one, it ate at him. During the long trip back to Rock Springs, he had lots of time to second-guess what he'd done. From a management point of view, he knew he'd done the right thing, but from a personal perspective, he wished he might have been able to handle it differently. The guy had family, and just turned fifty-three years old, a retired police officer, and a cancer survivor. Unfortunately, he had difficulty adhering to security policies. Three times he had violated the terms of CPI's contract with the federal government by allowing persons without clearances to enter missile silos in areas of restricted access. Under Federal Acquisition Regulations, Fred is obligated to report any contract violations to the facility's contracting officer, and even though Fred has already corrected the situation, he can expect a letter outlining the violations, to be a part of CPI's performance assessment.

When he arrived in Rock Springs he was exhausted, and Amy waited until the following day to bring him up-to-date. She first told him of the possibility that Tom Hastard might be involved in the missing bushing.

"Steve, Lolly came by and requested a copy of the logs showing who entered the site on the date the bushing disappeared," she told him.

"And you said?"

"And I said that I wouldn't give him the copies unless the CEO, Mr. McKinney, authorized me to."

"And he said?"

"He was a little taken aback, but I then told him that I would check the logs, and if there was anything there, I'd call him and the sheriff could call the CEO and request copies of the logs."

"What did you find when you checked the logs?"

Amy lifted the large desk calendar and took out several sheets of paper. They were copies of the logs that she had reviewed for Steve. She had highlighted a couple of entries in yellow. Tom Hastard had been logged into the site at 0012 hours on the eighth of February and had been logged out at 0420 hours.

"The sheriff did call the CEO and I got authorization to deliver copies of the logs to the sheriff's office, which I did."

"Why do they think Tom is involved?" Fred asked.

"Apparently, they were able to match some handwriting that was on some of the equipment logs and task orders," Amy replied.

"I get it," Fred commented, more to himself than to Amy. "They want those logs to ensure that they can put him on site where he had the opportunity to do whatever they think he did."

"I guess," Amy sort of agreed. "Now there is something else that I left for you to handle. The sheriff has asked for some help regarding surveillance activity. It is supposed to be done in the Farson area and we'd be working along with Ted Harper, the deputy for that region. You may wish to contact Ted to get the full story."

"I'll just head up that way, get him on the radio, and we can meet somewhere," Fred advised. "You don't need me here, do you?"

"Not today, but if things work out, I'll be transporting a person that's in emergency detention, to the Colorado border tomorrow." Amy proceeded to tell Fred about Dora, how she came to know her and that an active warrant was out on her. She also advised him that the SO was just waiting for paperwork authorizing the hold and the transport of Dora for an intercept by Colorado authorities somewhere close to the Wyoming-Colorado border.

As Fred passed through the town of Eden in his brown ford pickup with the CPI logo on the side, he tried contacting Ted on his Citizens Band radio instead of using the Motor Roller unit that had the sheriff's working channel on it. All the sheriff's patrol cars had CBs in them because most of the ranchers and all commercial truckers used them.

"Breaker, breaker, SO12-CPI 1 heading your way, come on."

"10-4 CPI-12, reading you loud and clear. Rendezvous country store in ten, come back."

"Roger, roger 12, make that 15. Out."

The Bronco with the sheriff's markings was already in the store's parking lot, backed in to a parking space and Fred pulled in beside him on the driver's side. They both wound their windows down.

"Either you're lost or Amy is really pod at you," Ted spoke first.

"Both," Fred replied. "She told me to get lost." They both chuckled. "They tell me that I might be able to give you a hand up here," Fred continued.

"I hope so, Fred. I really don't know what I've got but indications are that there may be an auto theft and chopping operation going on. The sheriff wants to set up surveillance on the suspected site. Can you help us?"

"Don't see why not. What are we looking for?"

"We want to record every vehicle that goes in and out of the old Boutros Ranch," Ted explained. "I'll show you where it is before you leave. We suspect that some that go in don't come out in one piece or may not come out in the same configuration that they went in. I also suspect that most of the movement takes place at night but we're going to watch it 24/7."

"How long do you anticipate pulling surveillance on the place?" Fred was beginning to think manpower requirements.

"I haven't had a chance to discuss that with the sheriff yet, but I'd look at a week for planning purposes, and then we'll go from there," Ted surmised. "If you're ready, I'll show you where the ranch is and then I'll show you the best spot to watch it from."

"Let's do it," Fred replied.

Ted led Fred across the main highway and on to the dirt road that accessed the ranch. He pulled off the road, stopping some distance from the gate. When they stepped out of the vehicles, they could just see the top of the big metal building.

"Okay," Ted began. "This is the place. That gate is always locked, so whoever goes in or out must stop and unlock it. That will give your people an opportunity to get descriptions and with a little luck, some license plate numbers. There's a main house on the property that you'll be able to see from the place I'm planning to set you up."

"How far away is this place we'll be watching from?" Fred was looking around and no position looked adequate.

"Get back in your pickup and let's get out of here before we're spotted," Ted said as he moved to his Bronco. "Follow me, I'll show you."

Ted pulled out onto the main road and headed south for about five hundred yards. He turned right onto a little used dirt lane that led to a small blue oval-shaped trailer nestled in a clump of pinion trees. The road ended on the west side of the trailer where there was a picnic table on a concrete pad. Fred and Ted exited their vehicles and walked up to the trailer door. Fred stopped and looked around. The spot was on a slight knoll and provided a clear view of the valley and the Boutros Ranch. Ted handed Fred a set of binoculars. After adjusting them to his eyes, Fred could see the front of the main house, the two overhead doors in the metal building, as well as the gate, clearly.

"Well, what do ya think?" Ted asked.

"This is perfect," Fred responded. "You own this?"

"No, no," Ted said with a smile. "The fellow that owns this is a wildlife photographer for one of those magazines like *Field and Stream* or something. He left for Alaska a couple of days ago. Whenever he travels, I watch his place. He'll be gone for a couple of weeks."

"I've got binoculars and spotting scopes and such, and I can get some night vision goggles and I have a camera with lenses that might come in handy," Fred advised. "What's inside?"

Ted took a key out of his shirt pocket and opened the trailer door. Fred looked in without going in. There was a bed, a table and bench, a sink, and a two-burner stove, and some cabinets. Just to the right of the door was a cabinet that had a plate that said furnace. There was also a window in the front facing the ranch.

"All the comforts of home, huh," Fred remarked.

"I thought you could make this work. Here's a key, just make sure your people take care of the place," Ted said.

"I'll be ready tomorrow evening and start operating the following morning. I'll have my guy here around 8:00 or 9:00 a.m. so that we don't alert anybody with lights and such. He will not be in uniform and the way these trees are situated, he can stay well obscured. I'll drop the second guy off about 6:00 p.m.," Fred advised.

As expected, Amy got the go ahead to transport Dora to the state line south of Laramie on Highway 287. Joyce, who had taken care of Sister Patricia Anne when she was in detention, was the most dependable, Amy thought, so she had taken her along to ride shot gun while she drove. Amy had a 1980 Tornado that she used for transports. It was roomy, comfortable, held the road well, and handled best at eighty-five to one hundred miles an hour.

Dora had switched personalities and was very cooperative as she was prepared for the trip. Amy didn't take any chances though, so she handcuffed her hands behind her back and put her in the back seat of the car. The Tornado was a two door so she wouldn't be able to get out if she did manage to get out of the seatbelt.

The trip was very smooth from Rock Springs to Rawlins. Dora conversed with Joyce most of the way. Sharing information about their families and places they had traveled over the years. As they were passing through Rawlins, there was a long period of silence. Just as they entered an area of construction where orange barrels were all over the place, all hell broke loose. Dora, now Doreen, drew her knees up to her chest and launched both feet against the back of Amy's head and let out a barrage of vulgarity as she reloaded and shot both feet against Joyce's head, striking her so hard that Joyce's seatbelt locked and she couldn't move forward away from the next onslaught. Amy maneuvered the car through the cluster of orange barrels out of traffic and stopped. She and Joyce, now free of her seatbelt, both entered the back of the car. Amy had grabbed several plastic ties from the pocket in the driver's door as she exited her seat. Joyce latched on to Doreen's legs at the knees and Amy threw her body on top of her torso, pinning her to the seat of the car. Doreen bit Amy right on the boob. She yelled for Joyce to help by rolling Doreen over on her stomach and Amy slipped a plastic tie through the cuffs. Joyce bent Doreen's feet toward her butt and Amy handed her a tie which she wrapped around Doreen's ankles and cinched it tight. Amy took a third tie and ran it through the tie on Doreen's wrists and through the tie on her ankles, slipped it through the anchor notch, and drew it tight. She instructed Joyce to help roll Doreen on the floor between the seats. Doreen ended up between the seats on her stomach trussed up like a turkey, screaming obscenities all the while.

While they stood catching their breath, Amy decided to check her boob. It was bruised but the skin wasn't broken. *Thank goodness for sports bras,* she thought. Other than being called several different kinds of whores, mother f****in bitches among a litany of other things, the rest of the trip was uneventful.

David Cooke was the co-owner of Ace Auto Recycling and South West Towing. His partner, Teddy Sturgis, ran the recycling portion of the business, an intrastate operation that through a unique network, supplied auto parts on request to automobile repair shops, auto restorers, dealers, and individuals throughout the country. Teddy had several employees whose job was to strip usable parts from salvaged vehicles, clean, catalog, and place them in inventory. Another crew was responsible to fill orders, pick from inventory, package, and prepare items for shipment using United Parcel Service.

David managed the towing operations. A very profitable relationship had been developed with most commercial carriers that ran the major highways leading east and west between Laramie, Wyoming, and the Utah border and north from the Rocksprings/Green River area to Jackson Hole/Yellowstone National Park region. There was lots of competition but between commercial trucks and travelers passing through on I-80 and tourist heading for Yellowstone, there was plenty of work for everybody, especially when the weather was bad.

Heavy duty towing equipment were prepositioned in Green River and Laramie to handle 18-wheelers on I-80 and smaller tow trucks with two-man recovery teams were positioned in Pinedale, Lander, Green River, Kemmerer, Casper, Greybull, and Gillette. Ace Recycling LLC was one well organized operation. Ever wonder how some operations maintain an adequate inventory of parts? Some purchase vehicles from owners that find it no longer economical to repair them; some purchase abandoned cars, pickups, and 18-wheeler tractors from storage yards; some even buy old vehicles at auction; and some are more opportunistic and along with routine methods of acquisition, engage in auto theft and chop operations.

David was not close to the Boutros side of the family but he became aware that there was going to be a sheriffs' sale while reading the local newspaper. He often scanned the legal section of the paper, looking for vehicles that might be for sale by banks and other financial institutions. He and his partner thought this was just what they needed. It was isolated and far enough off the main road that their activities would not attract attention. Ace Recycling was one of several interested parties but the others didn't want the property as badly as Teddy and David did.

Observing the ranch for the first couple of days was very unproductive. The only activity was David in his three-quarter ton Ford pickup. In the bed, a hoist had been mounted. When Fred viewed the pictures, he surmised that it might be used to lift engines.

Each day, Fred took the film to a photo shop and had it developed. The camera lens that was used provided clear images of the vehicle and the license plate. A check by the SO revealed that the vehicle was registered to David Cooke. On the fourth day of surveillance, at 4:40 PM, a gray Ford Aerostar van was observed entering the ranch. There were four occupants and the van was pulling a small trailer. On the trailer was a generator and what appeared to be a compressor. Using a handheld radio, the CPI observer could get the dispatcher at the SO to run the plate. The vehicle was registered to Ace Recycling. The van was observed being driven into the metal building. Shortly thereafter, the four occupants walked to and entered the main house. At 6:05 p.m., just prior to dusk, the truck registered to David Cooke left the ranch.

David Cooke drove north on Highway 191 to the town of Boulder located just a few miles south of Pinedale. There he met the recovery crew that operated out of Pinedale. A Ford F150 pickup was transferred from the crew's tow truck and hooked on to the back of David's truck using an A-shaped tow bar that hooked on to the front of the transferred truck. The license plate on the F150 was changed to one David had brought along. The transfer was made in all of three minutes and David headed back to Farson.

The population of boulder was approximately 170. Boulder proper sat back off the highway to the east and there was a small country store with a gas pump that was the only business next to the highway. To see a vehicle being retrieved along this stretch of highway would attract no attention at all.

At 8:27 p.m., David's truck was observed approaching the ranch gate with the F150 in tow. When he stopped to open the gate, the security person conducting surveillance took a picture of the truck and its license plate. When David approached the metal building, the overhead doors opened, both vehicles entered the building and the doors closed behind them.

Inside the building, the team that had come down from Kemmerer was waiting. The lighting in the building was not good because the fixtures were in the ceiling. The generator that had been brought powered lights that were positioned around the vehicle on stands. The compressor supplied the necessary pressure to operate power tools.

It was one of those crisp clear nights that can often be experienced in Wyoming. The moon, though high in the sky, bathed the valley with its light. At twenty-two minutes after midnight, the grey Aerostar van was seen exiting through the ranch gate. The trailer that had been towed by the van previously was not attached. With the help of the moonlight, the observer could clearly see through the camera lens that only three occupants were in the van. Fifteen minutes later, David Cooke's truck approached the gate towing a stock trailer.

The security officer watched the truck's headlights as it went to the main road, turned south, and then turned west onto a dirt road that would eventually come out on Highway 189 north of Kemmerer.

*****

The meeting room was well attended today. Sherrie, Steve, and

Kevin were there of course, but today there was Deputy Ted Harper from Farson, Fred Dreskel from CPI, and Don Rich, an investigator from the Wyoming Division of Criminal Investigations (WDCI) who had been invited by Ted. The DCI generally conducts criminal investigations at the request of local law enforcement agencies when it becomes apparent that criminal activity may cross jurisdictional lines. After going over the reports and pictures with Fred Dreskel pertaining to activity at the Boutros Ranch, Ted had considered the possibility that this might be the break DCI has been looking for. With Craig's permission, he had invited Don to be present.

"Good morning, team," Craig said as he entered the room and took his seat at the head of the conference table.

In chorus came the response, "Morning, Sheriff."

"Welcome, Fred," Craig continued. "To you, Mr. Rich, having you here is my pleasure. It's not often that we get an opportunity to rub shoulders with you folks in Cheyenne."

"It's great to get out here where the real work is done, Sheriff," responded Don Rich.

"What a politician," Craig quipped. "Okay, let's start by reviewing what we know about the activity out at the ranch. This whole thing came to our attention because of a vehicle ID plate found by Ted while trying to contact the new owner of the ranch. A check of that plate revealed that it belonged to a truck that had been reported stolen. Curious, I decided to put surveillance on the place for a short period to monitor any activity. Fred here has had people surveilling the place twenty-four hours a day for a week now. For your benefit, Mr. Rich, Fred here owns a security company that we use to augment our department. I'll let him relate what's been going on."

"Thank you, Sheriff," Fred began. "The first couple of days were very uneventful. The only movement was David Cooke leaving and entering the ranch." Fred stopped and passed some photos around the table depicting the truck that he said belonged to David Cooke, and then he continued, "On the fourth evening, a van shows up and it's pulling a trailer with a generator and a compressor on it." Again, Fred paused and passed out photos. "The license plate you see there registers to Ace Recycling out of Kemmerer. The van was driven into that large metal building you can see off in the distance in that picture I've just given you. Later that same evening, Dave Cooke drives out and heads north on Highway 191. After dark, around 8:30 p.m., he comes back towing a Ford F150 pickup. Here's a photo of his truck towing the pickup through the ranch gate. The pickup was towed right into the big metal building. The license plate on the Ford pickup was expired, issued out of Sublette County to a 1979 GMC Silverado. Shortly after midnight, the van leaves the ranch. There's only three people in it and it's not pulling the trailer. Shortly after the van leaves, David's truck leaves, there are two people in the truck, they're pulling a stock trailer. He goes out to the main road, turns right, and goes to Highway 28, which is a dirt road and heads west. As of today, the Ford F150 has not been driven from the ranch. So far, that's the only activity we've seen."

"Any guess as to what might have been in that stock trailer?" Craig asked.

"If they are doing what we think they're doing, I'd guess that that Ford pickup left the ranch in pieces, in that trailer," Fred commented.

"Why'd they bother to put an expired license plate on the truck?" Steve asked. "It was under tow, no one would pay any attention."

"If I were on patrol," Kevin spoke up, "and I saw a pickup, in good shape, no license plates, I think my curiosity would be tweaked quicker than one with a plate, I don't know, just saying."

"Well, Mr. Rice," Craig inquired, "what do you think?"

Rice leaned back in his chair and thought for a moment. He looked over the notes that he had taken on the matter, leaned forward, placing his elbows on the table supporting his chin with both fists, and spoke slowly, "There's nothing here that allows me to recommend to my boss that we should take action. However, we know something is going on and so far, this is the best lead we've had. I think I can convince the attorney general's office to commit resources and follow-up."

"My position is this," Craig began, "to my knowledge, there has been no theft of vehicles in Sweetwater County. I'm willing to help you people anyway I can, but I can't commit any more of my resources to build a case for you. When and if you determine that yep, there is a connection between the vehicle thefts in the state and the Boutros Ranch, and we have cause to believe a chop operation or some operation involving stolen vehicles is going on in this county, you can count on us to team up with you to take 'em down."

"That's fair enough, Sheriff. I'll get back to you folks in a couple of days and we'll go from there. Oh, and by the way, you can stop looking out for that informant in that camouflaged truck, we found him. A forest ranger came up on him and the truck in the hills west of Lander a couple of days ago. The snitch was there and he'd been shot right behind the right ear. The truck had been torched. The ATV that he always carried wasn't found though . . ."

One of David Cooke's associates was Dusty Weeks who had a background involving the theft of automobiles. Dusty was a tall, small-framed fellow, probably 6'4" and wirery. He had spent time in prison and had jailhouse tattoos on most of his upper body and arms. He didn't hide the fact that he'd done time when he was hired on. He was right upfront about being an ex-con.

During his interview, prior to him being hired, Dusty explained that he had grown up in Texas. He dropped out of high school and went to work at a private hunting ranch. His job was to keep the coyote population down so when he left, he kept on hunting and trapping them and learned to process the hides for sale to furriers.

While having a burger with Dusty in a local restaurant in Kemmerer, David was really interested in this hobby of Dust's and they agreed that Dusty would teach him. David also was interested in Dust's past.

"What happened to your job at the hunting ranch?" David asked.

"I got too chummy with the daughter of one of the hunting guides and got run off," Dusty replied with a chuckle.

"What did you do then?" David continued to inquire.

"Got hooked up with a smuggler and he taught me how to steal cars. Got pretty good at it."

"What did you do with the cars you stole?" David asked.

"We'd take 'em across the river into Mexico. There was a spot in the river that you could drive a car across most of the year. The guys on the other side of the river would have a car loaded with dope and we'd drive it back across to a used car lot that was a distribution point."

"What did you do when you couldn't cross the river?" David continued to pry.

"The used car place was also a chop shop so I would work there on off times."

"How'd you end up in jail?" David wanted to know, as he took another bite from his burger.

"DEA (Drug Enforcement Administration) figured out what was going on so they set up decoys with tracking devices in 'em. We ripped off one of the decoys and led them right to the spot where the deal went down. They didn't grab us until we picked up the car with the dope and got back on the US side. The Mexican Federal Police got the guys on the Mexican side. They busted the whole operation. They got me for grand theft auto, smuggling, transporting control substance, and a bunch other charges that they dropped because I plead guilty. In Texas, I could have gotten life for what we did. Instead, I was sent up for ten to twenty. They split us all up. Some went to Oklahoma to do time, some went of Kansas, Colorado, and I came to Rawlins."

"You spent twenty years in the can?"

"No. Overcrowding got a bunch of guys released early if they were in for a non-violent crime," Dusty said.

Over the coming days, David made several trips with Dusty to hunting spots, learning to set traps in some and moving to others where they shot an occasional coyote with a rifle. It was on one of these early morning hunts that David became suspicious of his newfound companion. They were traveling along a forest road when they came to a washout. The truck bounced and tossed as it crossed the ruts. Dusty had a clipboard that held maps of the area on the truck's dashboard and it went sliding toward the passenger side. Dusty tried to catch it but he missed and it ended up on the floorboard, at David's feet. The maps slid from under the clip. The only thing left clipped to the board was a card.

The card had a logo in the upper left corner, the logo of the Wyoming Division of Criminal Investigations. Without saying a word, David picked up the maps and clipped them back on the board, but his mind was racing a mile a minute. He thought to himself, *This guy got out early because he made a deal with the cops. I've got me a goddamn rotten snitch.*

He could hardly keep his wits about him. The road smoothed out and Dusty turned off into some low-lying bushes. He stopped the truck and got out, walked a short distance and stared down at the ground. There was a trap located there but there was nothing in it. When Dusty came back to the truck, he reached in the bed and took out a coffee can. "Want to smell something sweet?" he said to David, removing the top from the can. The can was full of rotted meat that was bait for the traps. "Some wily coyote got that bait without tripping the trap. These dogs are some kinda smart," he said as he was putting on a pair of rubber boots that he took from a tool box. He also took a plastic bottle of yellow-looking liquid from the box and squirted it on the soles of the boots before he put them on. The liquid was coyote urine and David could smell it even though Dusty was outside the truck. The urine would blot out the human smell.

After the trap had been rebaited, they drove to the top of an arroyo, where water from the hills around flowed through. Coyotes used the arroyo to move unseen through the area, and David intended to sit on the bank, concealed by sage brush, and pick them off as they came by.

They both took up positions with rifles at the ready. David found a clump of brush to the right and a little behind Dusty. The more he thought about what he'd seen in the truck, the more paranoid he became.

"There comes one," Dusty whispered, and crouched low in the weeds.

David looked in the direction that Dusty was looking and he could barely make out the animal trotting along close to the far bank some one hundred yards away. He watched Dusty slowly rest his elbow on his knee and bring his rifle to eye level. All his concentration was on the dog. He never saw David place his rifle a few inches from his head.

David placed Dusty in the truck behind the wheel, placed the metal ramps that Dusty carried in the back of the truck and backed the ATV off and out of the way. He then took a can of gasoline—Dusty always made sure he had plenty of gas—made sure the ATV's tank was full and drenched the interior of the truck. He then opened the hood of the truck and poured the remainder of the gas in the engine compartment. Standing on the ATV, he fired three rounds from his rifle at the engine block. The sparks ignited the fumes and the entire truck became engulfed in flames. As he mounted the ATV to leave, he gave Dusty the middle finger salute.

*****

"Holy shit!" Ted exclaimed. All heads turned in his direction. "Mr. Rice, you may have more than just stolen vehicles here," Ted continued. "When I met up with the owner of the ranch, he was riding a camouflaged four-wheeled ATV."

No one spoke. Everyone sat quietly, looking at one another. Rice sat with his mouth open and wide eyed. Ted went on, "The last time I saw that ATV, it was being driven into that big metal building on the property."

"Did you, by chance, document what you saw?" Rice asked.

"It's in my report, and it's also recorded because I told dispatch about the contact," Ted responded. "By the way, do you know what caliber was used to do the snitch?"

"There was no bullet found," Rice said. "It went in at an angle and came out above the left eye," Rice explained. "Why do you ask?"

"Because this guy, Cooke, the owner of the ranch, had what looked like a .38 revolver on him at the time we met."

"I'll check with the coroner and see if he was able to tell from the entry wound," Rice said as he took notes.

"Well, I guess you've got enough to chew on for now, Mr. Rice," Craig commented. "Thanks for stopping in. No, since you're hanging around for the rest of our meeting, sure you'd like to get cracking on this. Good luck to you."

"Sheriff, I really appreciate the invite. You guys do good work and I think we'll be doing business. Good day to you all," Rice said as he got up to leave.

After Mr. Rice had left the room, Craig complimented Ted and Fred on the work they'd done and then gave instructions. "Fred, you can pull your people off surveillance. If you would, I'd appreciate as much information as you can provide regarding the equipment you used on this job. If we ever do file a case, we'll need it, and give my thanks to your people. By the way, what is the status of that female with the two personalities you had in lockup?"

"Dora aka Doreen?" Fred said with a grin. "She was a fugitive from the state hospital in Colorado and they made arrangements to pick her up. So, with Sherrie's help, we got the necessary paperwork done and transported her to the Wyoming/Colorado border and turned her over to the Colorado State Highway Patrol."

"Good job," Craig said. "Let's move on and see what else we've got. Sherrie, whatcha got?"

"Believe it or not, things are very quiet. We'll have a few DWIs to escort to court and that's about it. There is one point of interest however. I dropped by the hardware store yesterday and saw Kenneth and visited with Mr. Tuber. Through the SWWRAP, Kenneth has a place to live, has a doctor that looks after his meds and stuff, and he's doing okay at the store."

"Next time I'm over that way, I'll try to look in on him," Craig said. "How about you, Kevin? How we doing on the brass ring?"

"It's all coming together, Sheriff. We got some help from the folks in Utah. They got the cooperation of Jackman Trucking and were able to lean on the driver that transported the bushing. He said that a guy that put the bushing on his truck also identified himself as the mine safety officer. The guy also told him that they were having trouble with the electric gate at the main entrance and it couldn't be opened right now, that they were working on it but it would be a while. He was escorted to another gate that allowed him to go out through the power plant. The driver said the safety officer called the security people on his radio and told them to let him through that way. He was also given a delivery slip with the address of a Metal Arts Foundry where he was to deliver the bushing." Kevin paused and took a photo out of a brown envelope and then continued, "They got to the foundry before they melted the bushing, and it's been secured as evidence. With Fred and Amy's help, we can put Tom Hastard on site at the time the bushing was taken and we believe he was the operator of the forklift that put the bushing on the truck."

"I think we've got enough to bring Hastard in and charge him," Craig surmised. "But before we do, since that bushing is still in one piece and can be retrieved, we'd better make sure that the mine wants to prosecute. It's been my experience with these big corporations that they really don't take kindly to putting their dirty laundry out for all to see. An arrest of a prominent employee such as Hastard would be pretty embarrassing."

After thinking over the situation for a moment, Craig turned to Fred. "Fred," he said, "you know these people much better than I, what do you think they'd want to do?"

"If there is any way possible, I think they'd take back the bushing and deal with Hastard in-house," Fred related.

"Okay," Craig leaned forward on the table and spoke to Kevin, "Let's do this. First, make arrangements to get that bushing back here. Then, get Hastard to come in. Lay it out for him. Let him know that we have two options. We can arrest him and charge him with theft, which in Wyoming, if the value of the property or services stolen is one thousand dollars or more, it's a felony and punishable by imprisonment for not more than ten years, a fine of not more than ten thousand dollars, or both; or he can tell us all about it and we'll give him the opportunity to explain to his superiors and we'll proceed based on their recommendations."

"What a deal," Kevin said. "I'd hate to have to choose."

"Fred, what do you think?" Craig asked.

"More than fair," Fred responded. "Plus, since the bushing has been recovered, I'm sure the corporation would rather handle things in-house."

"Steve?" Craig asked. "What do you think?"

"Boss, I say let's go for it," Steve responded. "If we can avoid putting this guy through the system and still close the case, it'll save us time and money."

"Okay," Craig agreed. "I'll get in touch with McKinney and brief him. He may want to be present when we talk to Hastard."

McKinney was an extremely tall man, an x-semi pro basketball player prior to becoming involved in coal mining; had bushy eyebrows, like those of John L. Lewis, the famous labor leader of the United Steelworkers Union, back in the day; had a full beard that was neatly trimmed and though Craig was not a fan of beards, he thought it was rather attractive. When McKinney entered Craig's office, he was still wearing his white hard hat that he's required to wear on the mine site. When he removed it to shake Craig's hand, a full head of steel gray hair was exposed.

"Sheriff Spence, Jeb McKinney," he introduced himself. "Great to finally meet you," he continued. "I was in a meeting when you called. My secretary tells me that there's some movement on the missing bushing."

"Good to see you too, Jeb," Craig responded. "It's not often that I get to meet the county's corporate neighbors unless they're bitching at me. Sit down, get a load off."

Craig removed a folder and large brown envelope from his desk drawer and placed them on top of his desk. "Before we get into this, I'm curious," he began, "if you would, enlighten me about this bushing. Why has it caused such a stir?"

"Well, the one that's missing is one of several that are in the inventory. It is a component of one of our drag lines. The drag lines are used to remove the overburden (dirt) and expose the coal veins in open pit mining operations. Simply put, the cab and power unit of this piece of machinery rides and rotates on this highly lubricated brass bushing. Over a period, this bushing wears to the point that it must be replaced.

When it's removed, it's then sent back to the manufacturer, refurbished, and returned to us to replace the next one that we remove. The one that's missing was to be shipped back for refurbishing."

"How did you happen to determine that it was gone?" Craig asked.

"Periodically, the purchasing department calls unannounced inventories that include the matching of shipping and receiving documents as well as the physical location of items," Jeb informed. "It was during such an inventory that we realized it was gone."

"Well, Jeb," Craig began. "I've got some good news and some bad news. Let's start with the good news first. The bushing has been recovered. We're in the process of returning it to this area as we speak."

Jeb made a motion as if whipping sweat from his brow. "I was really running out of time," Jed said. "It was fast reaching the point that I would have to notify corporate of the loss and the outcome would not be good. Now I can report that because of internal procedures, a theft was detected and with the help of local law enforcement, a monetary loss was averted."

"Your report may be impacted by the bad news," Craig commented.

"How so?" Jeb inquired.

"In this folder and envelope, we have information that gives us cause to believe that one of your employees was heavily involved in the removal of the bushing from the mine site."

"There was never a doubt in my mind that someone inside was involved, but I didn't have a clue. Who do you suspect?"

"I'm afraid it's past the suspect stage," Craig advised. "We know that Tom Hastard engineered this caper. We just don't know why for sure."

Craig let Jeb process what he'd just told him. They both sat in silence. Craig watched Jeb's face go from a show of strength to sagging like a scolded hound dog.

"I'm aware of the impact that an arrest of a member of your trusted management team will have within your operation," Craig went on. "The bushing will soon be back in your hands unless you wish us to prosecute. In that case, we'll have to hold it for evidence. To make matters worse, there is no way we can keep this from becoming headlines. Depending on how you wish to handle this will determine how the papers will report it. *Sweetwater County Sheriff's Deputies Arrest Security Manager at Sweetwater Mining Company for Theft of Mine Property,* with all the details, of course, or if you'd like to handle this in-house, an article on page six will read, *Sweetwater County Sheriff's Deputies Assist Local Mining Company to Locate Missing Property.* Which one do you like?"

Before Jeb could answer, the phone rang. It was the interoffice line.

"Spence," he said turning away so that his back was to Jeb. It was Steve on the line.

"Say, boss," he said, "we've got Hastard here in the office. He's a mess. He almost seems relieved that we found him out. Which way do we handle this?"

Craig turned back to face Jeb as he said to Steve, "Let me get right back to you."

Craig hung up the phone and again spoke to Jeb. "We've got your man downstairs. He's broke up about it but he may be glad it's over. It's your call, sir."

"You know," Jeb began, "when you run an outfit the size of Sweetwater Coal, with over one thousand three hundred employees, you hear a lot of yak, yak, about people and you don't pay a lot of attention to it. As I sit here and think back, maybe I should have checked some of it out. He's a good employee, a great safety man. It's most likely that he's got a problem and I missed it. We have programs that we can put an employee through to help them. Thanks to you and your people, we may be able to save a man's career. I'd like to take him back with me, Sheriff. How can I ever thank you?"

"Not me, Jeb. Two guys that take their jobs seriously," Craig said. "Tell you what, every year the SO conducts safety classes in all the elementary schools in the county. We generally do them on Saturdays so we can have hotdogs and hamburgers after. If you are interested in being a sponsor, I can have one of the deputies get a hold of you when they conduct the next one."

"Deal," Jeb almost shouted as he reached across the desk to shake Craig's hand.

Craig punched the intercom button on his phone that connected to Steve's office. "Steve, come to my office and bring our guest."

At the end of the day, Craig felt that he and the department had had one of those rare periods when everything that they had been faced with had a positive outcome. Craig reached in the upper right draw of his desk, took out a flask and a plastic cup. He poured two fingers of bourbon in the cup, replaced the flask, closed the drawer, and sat back in his chair. That first sip felt good going down. It warmed his insides. He took the quite time to reflect on recent events and outcomes.

What a rough time Kenneth Boutros must have had over the years, Craig thought. He wasn't in Vietnam for any patriotic reasons, he was just doing a job, but he left a part of himself there on behalf of this country nonetheless. He was thrown back into a world he was no longer equipped to deal with and every time there was an opportunity to provide some support for him, the system, intentionally or not, failed him. Craig wondered, *had Kenneth Boutros been functioning at full mental capacity, could he have mustered the strength to endure the disappointments, frustrations, and feelings of abandonment? Was it not for that injury, which left him somewhat diminished, could it have been too much for him to bear and he'd have become just another statistic?* Craig took another sip of bourbon.

There was Stacy Cappers. Craig could still visualize him lying in that hospital bed a few months back when he had to tell him his mother was dead. He was in bad shape but alive. A guy, Albert Brown, that had killed his partner in the county jail, escaped and was on the run when he had come across Stacy and his mom. Brown killed the old lady and he thought he had killed Stacy too and buried him in a shallow grave. Brown had taken the couple's car and somehow avoided the net law enforcement agencies had setup to aid in his capture. Craig opened his center desk drawer and took out the map he had used to anticipate Brown's escape routes. He smiled as he recalled the events of the tracking, the chase, and the final cornering. Kevin had been wounded in the ensuing gun fight and Craig, luckily, was able to take Brown out. *I wonder what happened to Stacy,* Craig thought, as he sipped and returned the map to the drawer. He recalled that the coroner's inquest and review by the state's attorney general's office of his causing the demise of Brown, justified.

Then there was Sister Patricia Anne. That little lady was some kinda lucky. She could have been killed out there on the highway, but wasn't. She could have frozen to death, but didn't. She could have ended up in a looney house or dead, but for a doctor's curiosity, she didn't. And she survived and has a chance to mend.

Norman Gaither, the oil field worker who raped the twelve-year-old girl in Bairoil, really didn't have to die even though he deserved to. *His decision to take me out,* Craig thought, *sealed his fate. It was him or me, and I like the way it turned out,* he thought.

After much consternation and concern about what the ACLU was going to do to us, it looks like they have been held at bay and a new detention complex could be in the making. Craig smiled to himself and downed the last of the bourbon. *It's been a good couple of months,* he thought.

Craig took a tissue from a box of Kleenex on the desk, and wiped the inside of the plastic cup before putting it back in the drawer. He picked up the handset from its cradle on the phone and punched the intercom button. "Sherriff Spence is leaving the building. Good night."

CHAPTER

It's March and South-Eastern Wyoming is beginning to warm up. The average temperature is forty-eight degrees Fahrenheit and more days are partly cloudy instead of gray and overcast. There is now a forty-two percent chance that there may be some type of precipitation at some point in every day; the most likely type of precipitation being snow flurries. The average wind speed during the month is usually twenty-three miles per hour, constantly, and periods of calm occurring only when the wind is changing direction. The residents of the area are looking forward to spring.

Traffic along I-80, other than 18-wheelers, picks up in March; tourist heading to the west coast or north to the national parks in northern Wyoming and Montana. Job seekers begin to flow into the county seeking employment in the mines or gas and oil fields. Based on his experience from previous years, Craig knew that there would be an increase in the populations of the county's towns and villages from now until fall, boosting the workload on his people and would stretch the capacity of the jail to its limits.

Unfortunately, there had been some hiccups in the plans to construct a new detention facility. The city of Green River had contested the site that had been selected and filed suit against the county. According to a law that was still on the books, the county jail had to be located at the county seat. The site which had been selected was on county owned property outside the limits of Green River, the county seat. Because of the delay, the ACLU had refiled its suit and Craig was forced to reduce the number of inmates housed at any one time to sixty-five and any overflow had to be detained in the facilities of other counties that had already constructed new facilities or modified existing centers to satisfy previous ACLU suites. The county commissioners had petitioned the state legislature to change the law. In the meantime, prisoners that exceeded the sixty-five number had to be transported out of county. Again, the arrangement with CPI came in to play and most transports were accomplished by them. The impact on the department's budget was substantial and Craig used the forced expenditures as the basis to request a supplemental increase to his department's budget. Under the circumstances, his request was approved with no resistance from the commissioners.

Prior to leaving for work each morning, Craig routinely had a couple cups of coffee. This morning, for the first time since her operation, Martha joined him.

"Morning, doll," he said as she sat at the table across from him. "Sorry if I woke you when I got up."

"No, no," she said through a yawn. "Nature called and I smelled the coffee. Sure smelled good. Got enough for another cup?"

"You betcha," he said as he got up to get a cup. "Nice having your company to start my day. You got anything special planned for the day?"

"I think I'm going to have Katie take me shopping. Spending some of your money will do wonders for my disposition," she said with a big smile.

"Never thought I'd say this, but that's a great idea," Craig said as he placed a cup of coffee in front of her. "I'm so pleased that you're going to get out and about."

"Been housebound long enough," she said and took a sip of her coffee. "I might even take in a movie."

"Hey! No fair," Craig exclaimed. "What's playing?"

"I understand *The Last of the Unicorns* is in town. Want we should wait till you come home and we can go together?"

"I'd like that. I'll even take you to dinner afterward," he said as he got up to leave. He leaned over and gave Martha a kiss on the forehead. “I’ll try to get home early. Have fun shopping,” he said over his shoulder as he went out the door.

*****

The coming of summer had an impact on business at the salvage yard in Kemmerer too. There was always an uptick in the demand for auto parts and accessories this time of year—bumpers, quarter panels, grills, hoods, windshields, doors, and main frames, as wells as transmissions, transfer cases, gear boxes, and engines. There were several reasons for the high demand for parts. First, after the winter months pass, and ice and snow conditions are less frequent, people begin to seek repairs of damages that occurred from road crashes on icy highways. Wind conditions, blowing small stones, and sand across highways and 18-wheelers propelling rocks take a heavy toll on auto glass, and severe temperatures, often twenty degrees and below, is responsible for damage to engines and some accessories. Second, during the spring and summer, off-road enthusiast convert pickups and some cars to off-road vehicles. Third, because of the harsh conditions, many car and truck owners are reluctant to buy new vehicles, but are content to upgrade the one they have instead. Inventories at parts stores and body shops were strained.

The demand for parts was such that Teddy Sturgis, part owner of ACE Salvage and South West Towing, had to put on extra help, three extra men in the yard stripping parts and two females part-time; one to help with cleaning and packaging for shipping, and the other to pick parts in the stock room.

David Cooke, the other half of the partnership, was being hard pressed to keep the salvage yard supplied. He and his tow teams had to work a wide area of the state so as not to put too much pressure on any one area. One thing in their favor was that during the spring and summer months, all counties and towns of any size sponsored fairs and rodeos. When these events were going on, pickings were pretty good. Lots of cars and trucks came in from locations other than where the events were being held, vehicles were coming and going most of the time, and very little attention was paid to activities along the access roads and parking lots. People attending the events were more apt to be careless or completely distracted most of the time, making it easy to select, hot wire, and drive off unnoticed.

Another source was cars and pickups that had been temporarily left along the highways by their owners. During regular operations, David had his tow crews look out for cars and trucks that had been left along the roadways and tagged by the highway patrol. If a vehicle is not a danger to traffic, law enforcement will generally attach a bright orange or green tag. This means that the owner has twenty-four to forty-eight hours to move it. Anyone seeing a tow truck hooking up a vehicle so tagged would think nothing of it.

It was the beginning of May that Craig received a phone call from Don Rice at the Wyoming Division of Criminal Investigation. Though there had been no reported auto thefts reported to his department, Craig had often wondered what was going on with the investigation by the state.

"Spence here," Craig answered the phone.

"Afternoon, Sheriff, Don Rice at WDCI. Is this a secure line?"

"Only that it's my private line and few people have the number. With that in mind, go ahead."

"We're setting up a meeting with local enforcement agencies from whom we'll need assistance when we conduct specific operations. The purpose of the meeting is to coordinate events. The meeting will be held at our offices here in Cheyenne on May 4 at 8:00 a.m. Can you make it?"

Craig looked at his desk calendar and saw that the date was just two days away. *Things must be about to go down pretty quick,* he thought.

"I'll see to it that someone from the department is there," Craig assured him.

"Thanks, Sheriff. Looking forward to working with you," Don said before he hung up.

Craig decided to send Kevin to Cheyenne. His leg had healed nicely and he wasn't tied up with anything.

*****

Kevin drove up to Cheyenne the night prior to the meeting and was one of the first to arrive at the WDCI building in the morning. Representatives from other counties began to trickle in as it got closer to the meeting time. Sheriff's departments from Carbon, Laramie, Freemont and Lincoln, Sublette, Uinta, and Sweetwater counties were represented.

All seated themselves at a large conference table in the center of the meeting room. In the front of the room was a mobile electrical cart with equipment used to operate an overhead projector. A large white screen hung from the ceiling and covered the wall directly in front of the projector. A podium was positioned off to its left. Agent Rice did not disappoint. Right at 8:00 a.m. he entered through a side entrance near the front of the room and took his place at the podium.

"Good morning all," he said as he looked out at the gathering and there was a chorus of recognition from the attendees to his greeting. Then he continued, "Welcome to WDCI. The information you receive today and topics discussed must be held in strictest confidence and conveyed only to those individuals in your departments with a need to know." He paused to give his comments an opportunity to settle in. "As each of you is aware, there has been a rash of auto thefts reported throughout the state over the past few months. After following up on information provided us by the Sweetwater County SO, we have been working on the assumption that there might be an organized ring operating. Our motor vehicle investigators confirmed our suspicions and informed us that the department had made some effort, over the past year, to infiltrate the operation. In fact, they had successfully placed an operative inside but something went wrong and he ended up dead. We managed to convince the attorney general to make the investigation a priority . . .

"The investigators started by reviewing the files the department had on Ace Auto Recycling. Auto recycling and other auto salvage yards are required to submit a monthly report to the state. This is generally a pass-through report to the National Motor Vehicle Title Information System (NMVTIS). Data regarding vehicles processed by the facility such as the type and model, the vehicle's VIN (Vehicle Identification Number) which has been assigned by the manufacturer. The date the vehicle was obtained and the individual or entity from whom it was obtained, and the way a vehicle was disposed of, was the basis for actions that followed.

"Six months of reports submitted by Ace Recycling was reviewed by the investigators. Thirty-seven reports were reviewed by the investigators. Of those, seventeen were found to have information that got their attention, such as VIN with only fifteen or sixteen digits when there should be seventeen; or type of vehicle information did not match a VIN code.

"With the help of the state's Department of Motor Vehicles, information contained in the reports submitted by Ace Recycling was cross-referenced against information available in Department of Motor Vehicle's files. In several cases, the person that Ace reportedly obtained the vehicle from was not the last person to register it. When the proper VIN was matched to an individual, attempts were made to contact the last person that registered the vehicle. The team successfully contacted six persons. In each case the owners had reported their vehicle stolen. One owner informed the investigators that he had etched the first four and last eight digits of his F250 Ford truck's VIN on all saleable accessories and components that he could get to. He had come from the Texas Panhandle where it was not uncommon to fall victim to car thieves, however, his truck had been stolen from Ten Sleep, Wyoming, while attending a rodeo.

"Though the state is required to periodically inspect auto recycling and auto salvage yards, inspections are infrequent unless there are complaints. Because of the inconsistencies noted during the current investigation, the Motor Vehicle Department decided an inspection to be warranted and useful in collecting information. Ace had not been inspected for four years . . ."

Everyone sat attentively waiting for Rice to divulge what had been found. He paused for a moment and picked up the remote control for the projector. An image appeared on the large screen on the wall.

"This is a picture of the underside of the right quarter panel, above the right front wheel of a stripped car that had been in the yard for some time. During the inspection, an investigator was able to scrap away enough of the rust and dirt to expose the VIN of the vehicle." Moving to the projector, Rice took a pen and pointed to a series of numbers faintly visible in the image. Then he continued, "This vehicle was a 1979 Nissan, reported stolen by the Lander Wyoming Police Department over two years ago. The VIN for that Nissan was reported on a submitted report for a 1979 Camry that was totaled on Highway 191 a couple of years back. We suspect that the Camry's VIN plate ended up on some other car some place." Rice flicked the remote and the image on the screen changed, and he continued, "This shows a radiator bracket that our investigator found on a trailer with some other assorted metal. Notice in the upper left corner of the bracket," he again pointed with his pen. "There are several numbers. Remember, I earlier told you that a victim had said that he etched parts on his truck? Guess what, the numbers on this bracket matched."

Rice returned to the podium. "During the MVD people's inspection," agent Rice continued, "there were enough pieces of evidence noted that our investigators were convinced that there was indeed an illegal operation at play. They managed to get one of their agents hired on part-time at the Kemmerer salvage yard. We've been informed that on this coming weekend, the employees at the Kimmerer location will be working day and night on vehicles that have been hidden in various locations and will be delivered to the salvage yard on Saturday evening. That's two days from now. I realize that this is short notice, but it's our best shot at taking these people down. There's one other part to this. Our undercover agent has been tasked to pick up a white Ford van in Thermopolis and drive it to the Boutros Ranch. The information we have obtained is that the van is to be stripped and modified for transporting drugs. The drug enforcement people have been notified but aren't interested in getting involved. Here's our plan."

Rice went on to explain that there were stash locations in Natrona, Carbon, Sublette, and Uinta counties and that WDCI plans to descend on each of them at 2:00 a.m. on Sunday morning. He advised that WDCI lacked the personnel to conduct the operation on its own and that the help of county law enforcement would be needed to support the operation.

"We'll have one agent at the respective county headquarters prior to "0" hour with search warrants in hand," as he spoke, Rice reached under the podium and took out several brown envelopes and handed the first one marked Natrona County to the officer representing that county prior to continuing to speak. "We are sure that by the time we make our move, any cars or trucks will already be at Kemmerer or on the way there. That's okay. In the envelope I've given you is a listing of items that were in the vehicles that were stolen in your county to include the make, model, and VIN of the vehicles that we believe were hidden there. I have an envelope for each of you with like information so you'll know what we're looking for. There are also names of persons that we expect will be on the premises. There will be warrants for those persons also."

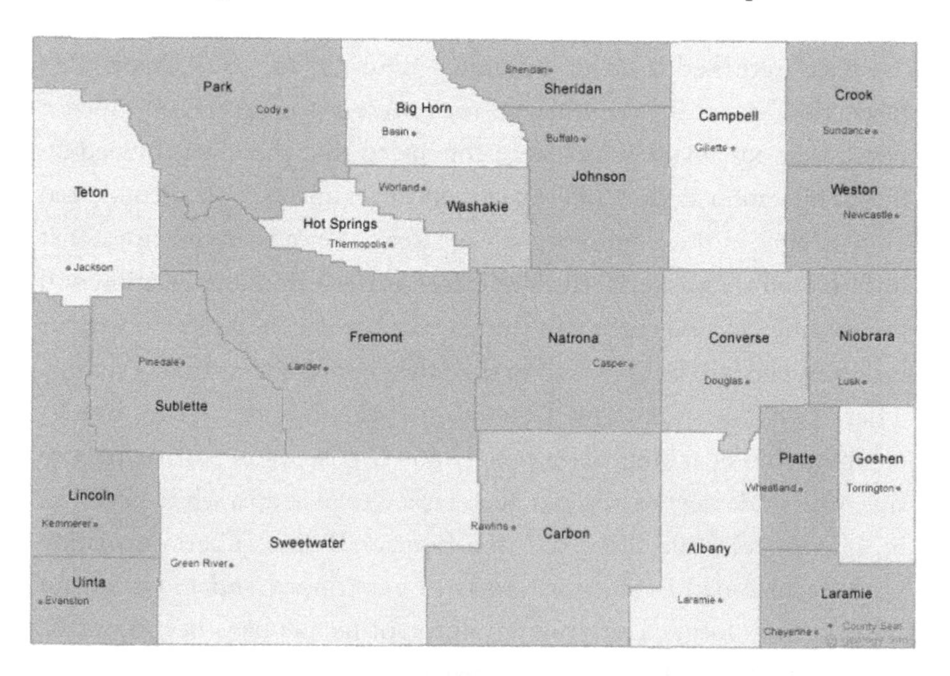

"In Lincoln County, we'll have several of our agents at your offices at 1:00 a.m. We will need the help of the Lincoln County SO to conduct a blocking operation and assist with containment and securing evidence. The agents will have the necessary warrants. The same assistance will be needed from the Sweetwater SO with one exception. That van will be driven by our guy. When he stops the van at the gate, two of our agents, along with a couple of your people, will get in the van. The van is a conversion type and has cargo doors so entry will be easy. It has curtains at the windows and drapes that close off the front from the cargo section. Our guy will have a key to the gate lock and you'll be driven right up to the building. Everyone except the driver will get out and take cover. When the door is opened for the van to enter, we'll follow the van inside, announce ourselves, and keep everyone in place." Kevin spoke up.

"Mr. Rice, we know that David Cooke is armed and may have already killed. What's your plan once inside, to isolate him?"

"Thanks for bringing that up," Rice responded. "Cooke will be our guy's responsibility. He knows who he is by sight and he'll seek him out and take him out of action. We don't know how many people in that building may also be armed so make sure your men are aware of the possibilities, and one more thing, we want complete radio silence from the people involved in the operation from midnight until contact is made at each location and the agent in charge will give a status report. These people probably monitor our channels."

The meeting lasted several additional hours involving the county representatives being introduced to WDCI, people that will participate in the operation and kicking around possible plan Bs in case things don't go as anticipated. One of the concerns was, what if someone makes a run for it, do they give chase or what? Rice responded to that concern.

"We are interested in corralling two people," he began. "Teddy Sturgis at the Kemmerer operation and David Cooke at the ranch in Sweetwater County. If any of the crew members pose a danger to our people, we take them down or take them out. If they just rabbit on us, let them go and officers providing containment on the perimeters can deal with them."

It was late in the day when Kevin returned to the sheriff's office. He went straight to Craig's office where he spent an hour or so briefing him about the upcoming operation. Craig was none too happy about having to rush to support WDCI's plan.

"One of the things I've learned over the years is that piss poor planning leads to piss poor performance," Craig related to Kevin. "I always get a knot in my gut when there are a bunch of unknowns, like how many people are we dealing with at the ranch? How many exits are there to that building? What about the house? How many escape routes are there? We've got some planning to do and we've got less than twenty-four hours to get it done. Have dispatch contact all deputies not on duty tomorrow and have them report here at 6:00 a.m. I'm going to call the airport and see if the manager can fly me over the ranch for a look see."

At day break, Craig was airborne. Visibility was great and he could see for twenty miles or so. The pilot didn't have to fly directly over the ranch to see the lay of the land. As they flew north along the ranch's east boundary, Craig could see the entrance gate, the yard between the house, and the metal building, the overhead door at its east end, and the fence connected to the entrance gate, and enclosed what had been the headquarters of the ranch. Craig had the pilot make a wide turn and fly along the west boundary and he could see the trails made by the sheepherder wagons and other vehicles as they left the ranch through an opening in the fence, over a cattle guard, split and headed north and west into the foothills, where the sheep were grazed during the spring and summer months. The trail going west curved back and forth along the base of the foothills till it reached Fontanelle Dam that he could see in the distance.

On the west side of the metal building was another overhead door. There was a white horse trailer backed up to the door and there were sheep pins on that side of the building filled with tires, old vehicle bumpers, and other discarded vehicle carcasses. There was an item parked beside the horse trailer that really caught his eye—a four-wheeled camouflaged ATV.

Seven off duty deputies, SO9, SO10, SO6, 8, 5, 12 and 14, including Steve, Kevin, and Ted, showed up at 6:00 a.m. and were in the conference room when Craig returned from his flight. He took his hat and placed it on the table and pulled up a chair. "I need volunteers for a special job in cooperation with the Wyoming Department of Criminal Investigations," he said as he looked around the table. He was not surprised when all ten raised their hands. "Kevin," he said, "give everyone a rundown on what's going to go down."

As Kevin spoke, everyone listened intently. As he outlined the mission, all at the table seemed to become more and more enthralled with what was about to happen. They hadn't had such excitement in most of their careers. When Kevin had finished, Craig reached into the breast pocket of his shirt and took out a folded sheet of paper. He opened it up and flattened it out on the table.

"Gather round," he said. During his flight, he had made a rough sketch of the layout of the ranch. He continued, "Our first objective is to setup a blocking situation in case some make a run for it out the back door." With his finger, he pointed to his sketch. "On the northwest portion of the perimeter fencing, there is the only opening that a vehicle could get through. My concern is that someone might try and use an ATV to get out into the country side. I saw one behind the metal building. SO9 and 10, about midnight, I want you guys to hike in from Ted's place about a mile north of the ranch. All you have to do is head south down the valley and you run into the fence. Shouldn't take you more than about thirty to forty-five minutes. Find the opening and standby. Should someone head out that way, you'll be notified on our radio channel two." With his finger, he again pointed to the sketch and continued. "SO6, there's a small ditch about one hundred yards south of the gate. I want you to slither under the fence there and position yourself so you can watch the back of the house. There is nothing but sage brush between you and the house so you don't have to worry about obstacles. Steve, Ted, and I will climb over the gate and position ourselves so we can watch the front of the house, any vehicles in the yard, and the front of the metal building. After midnight, the moon will be high so we should get some help seeing." Craig paused, folded the paper, and spoke directly to the rest of the group. "SO8, 5, 12, and 14, you guys will be the assault team along with the WDCI agents in the van. We'll all, except SO9 and 10, meet up with them in the parking lot of the Farson Store at 1:00 a.m. As soon as I get out of here, I'll brief agent Rice so that we'll all be reading off the same sheet. Anybody got a question?" No one spoke up and Craig ended the meeting with, "Go home and get some rest, see you tomorrow morning."

*****

There was a moon as the team began to gather, but it was also partly cloudy and there was a mild breeze. As the clouds moved across the sky, there were periods when the moon was shielded. Craig thought this condition was in their favor, because they could coordinate their movement with the moon being behind the clouds. At 1:30 a.m., everyone spread out and began moving toward the ranch's gate.

The Lincoln County sheriff's office had the salvage yard under surveillance all night. One pickup had been driven through the gates about midnight and a sedan entered shortly thereafter. The observer was using a warehouse directly across the street from the yard for concealment. At 1:30 a.m., a GMC Yukon with a WDCI agent and three deputies pulled in behind the warehouse. From the corner of the warehouse, using binoculars, the agent could see through the office window over the top of three cars parked in front. The office was a double wide mobile home. The shop area was behind the office. He could see someone, a male, on the phone, and he seemed to be agitated. The person threw the phone down and ran to a door at the back of the office.

"Something's up," the agent said. "Let's go," he shouted.

The Yukon was driven to the gate. One of the two deputies aboard climbed atop the Yukon, threw a tarp across the barbed wire that topped the gate, and they both crossed over into the yard. The overhead door at the back of the shop was opening and people were coming out.

"Sheriff's office, everybody freeze!" The deputies shouted as they drew their guns.

The agent and the deputy that had been watching the yard forced their way through the office door and were immediately confronted by two males heading out that way. The agent held his gun in one hand and held up his badge with the other. The deputy also had his gun out as the agent spoke, "Police! You're under arrest!"

There was a waiting area of sorts on one side of the room and the two individuals were directed to sit.

"Which of you is Mr. Sturgis?" the agent asked. There was no response. One of the men the agent recognized as the man that had been on the phone. He was pretty clean and his hands looked like they hadn't done any hard work. His shirt was starched and his jeans were high dollar. He wore a cap that read: Ace Auto Recycling, on the front. The agent took some papers out of his hip pocket and approached the man wearing the cap.

"Stand up and face the wall," the agent commanded. He conducted a frisk procedure and removed a wallet from the man's jeans. The driver's license was issued to Theodore Sturgis.

"Mr. Sturgis," the agent began. "Please sit down, sir. This is a search warrant for this location; all buildings, vehicles, shacks, and property enclosed by that fence and identified as Ace Auto Recycling. I also have an arrest warrant for you and I intend to detain and take all persons on the property into custody." The agent proceeded to handcuff Teddy. The deputy searched and handcuffed the other party, they were then cuffed together, back to back.

Entering the shop area, the agent saw that the other deputies had four male individuals and one female handcuffed on the floor. In the work bay, there was a Toyota Camry on jacks, partially dismantled and a Ford pickup with a cherry picker hooked to its engine.

Sturgis had been alerted that there was trouble. When the Sublette County sheriff's deputies moved in on a garage just outside of Pinedale, the target spotted them and bolted to a nearby trailer park, where he barricaded himself in a trailer and called Sturgis to warn him that the cops were there.

The van pulled up to the Boutros Ranch gate a little before 2:00 a.m. The driver (undercover agent), got out, leaving the vehicle's bright lights on, which not only provided added illumination on the gate's lock, but also prevented anyone who might be watching from the house or metal building, to see the deputies scurrying to enter the van through the side and back cargo doors. The interior of the van was equipped with bench seats along the sides instead of captain's chairs and the group easily fit with each man on his knees facing the way he would exit. After securing the gate, the driver proceeded slowly down the road toward the house and metal building. Craig and his team waited until the van was almost at the building before they began their trek. As they approached the front of the metal building, the driver spoke for the first time, "Ah shit," he said. "There's two guys out front. Looks like they may be smoking. Don't move, anybody. Don't want this buggy to rock."

Someone whispered with some anxiety in his voice, "I'm getting a cramp!"

Another voice, also in a whisper, "Suck it up!"

As the van was brought to a stop, the driver rolled down his window and motioned to the two for somebody to open the overhead door. The person closest to the van walked over to the personnel entrance, reached in, and apparently pushed a button because the door began to go up. As soon as the van could clear the rising door, it was moved into the building and the door could be heard to stop and reverse itself, shutting them in. Quietly, the driver spoke again. "There's three guys. They're standing together. One is motioning me to go to a spot near some lights. You guys going out the side will be closest to them. On my call, bail."

The van is brought to a stop and the driver yells, "Go! Go! Go!"

The van's doors flew open and lawmen leap out the side and back on the run, quickly surrounding the startled threesome.

The two men that were outside had entered the building behind the van and were now headed out the personnel door. SO5, apparently the team member with the cramp, was limping toward them as they disappeared out the door.

One man, after exiting the building, headed toward the house, the other made a dash around the side of the metal building toward the back.

"Freeze! Sherriff's office!" Ted was yelling at the individual heading to the house. Instead of stopping, he darted around the west side of the house out of sight. Steve, having given chase toward the rear of the building, heard the ATV crank up and sped off into the night just prior to him getting back there.

"We've got rabbits!" Craig was on his radio. "SO6, one's coming your way, Nine. Ten, ATV headed your way."

A shot split the night quiet. Everybody froze, including Steve who had worked his way to the sheep pens west of the house. The sound came from SO6's location. Several seconds passed and all was quiet.

The last ten years that SO6, Harry Kushner, had been with the department ran through Craig's mind. Harry had joined right out of the service and had a prosthetic leg. He could out walk or run circles around most of the younger guys. He married his wife, Susan, just a couple of years ago and she had a young daughter from a previous marriage that Harry loved dearly. Harry was one of those guys that was dedicated and always ready to fill in if there was a need. Craig couldn't wait any longer. "SO6 this is One, speak to me." There was no response.

Ted and Craig, using the house as a shield, crouched and moved in the direction that the shot had come from. Craig called again, "Harry, you okay?"

Gasping for breath, Harry responded, "Jumped him . . . but he pulled a revolver . . . got busy trying to take it . . . it went off . . . managed to open cylinder and dump ammo . . . he got away."

"Where's he headed?" Craig asked.

"To the sheep pens . . . he's got no bullets."

"Everybody listen," Craig said over the radio, "be careful. He may have reloaded. Steve, where are you?"

"I see him," came a whisper in response. "He's coming right at me. Can't tell if he's still got the gun."

Steve crouched behind a twelve by six corner post like an animal ready to spring. He watched the person stumble up the path between his position and another sheep pen. He was breathing hard and coughing. As he passed, Steve sprung, driving the man forward and into the dirt. Steve wasted no time pinning his arms behind him and cuffing him. There was no more fight in him. The guy just laid there, trying to catch his breath. There was spittle running out the sides of his mouth into his thick brown beard. Steve proceeded to search his captive, checking every inch of his body and all his pockets. He found the revolver in his pant pocket. It was empty.

"Man in custody," Steve said over the radio.

It wasn't long before Craig and Ted joined him. Craig patted him on the back and through a big smile was complimentary. "Great job, Steve, great job."

Craig moved a few feet away and again spoke into his radio, "SO9 and SO10, status?"

"This is Nine, one in custody. He tried to run through a barbed wire gate across the trail and the gate won."

"10-4," Craig responded. "One of you bring that ATV with you. The state investigators may be interested in it."

Moving back to where Ted and Steve stood with their captive, Craig asked a question to which the answer brought another big smile to his face.

"Who we got here, fellows?" Ted made the introduction.

"Sheriff Spence, meet Mr. David Cooke."

CHAPTER 10

It was Mother's Day and Craig was pleased to have time to devote to Martha. They spent the morning just lounging in bed, after enjoying a breakfast of waffles and eggs that Katie had prepared for them. An emotional moment caused Martha to tear up when Katie entered the bedroom with a beautiful bouquet of assorted roses—pink, yellow, and red—with a card attached that read simply, "To MOM, on your day, from Katie and Dad."

It had been a tough few weeks for Martha. The radiation treatments had zapped all her strength and stamina. Just recently, she had developed a cough which she had been told might happen because the treatment was directed at the chest area. Prior to the cough was the itching. There were times when she wanted to just dig her fingers into the skin and rake until the skin was all gone.

Craig had been wonderful through it all. Not only did he continuously put moisturizing creams and lotions on her skin, which by the way did not stop the itching, but kept the skin from drying up and it felt good. Craig helped in another way. He allowed her to talk about how she felt. He wanted to know what was going on, what she was going through, what she felt physically and emotionally. Talking about this thing, this cancer that brought her life to a virtual standstill, his interest helped her deal with being disfigured, helped her deal with the uncertainties of the eventual outcome, and helped her deal with the occasional desire to just die.

"You know what I'd like to do?" Martha said, as she reached over and took Craig's hand in hers.

"This is your special day," Craig replied. "Anything you wish, doll."

"I'd like for you to drive me over to Expedition Island where I can watch the Otters play and the kids trying their luck at fishing, and where you and I can just sit and spend some quiet time together."

"You think we oughta get dressed first?" Craig quipped.

"You know what I meant." Martha pulled his hair causing his head to rest against her chest and she rubbed it with her fist until he let out a yelp from the burn.

<u>Expedition Island Park</u>

Expedition Island was a well-kept park that sat in the middle of the Green River where it entered and meandered through the town. The island was historic because many expeditions down the river had been launched from there. The river boiled up on both sides and made for kayaking, tubing, floating, and some pretty good fishing. On hot days, there was always a cool breeze across the island.

The sun was high in the sky when they arrived at the park. They found a shady area where the river split and engulfed the island. There was no bench, so they lounged on the grass, he sitting, using one arm to support him upright and she, lying with her head in his lap, looking up and admiring the cloud formations as they drifted across the sky. They remained this way for a long time until Craig broke the silence. "Do you realize we haven't been together like this since before we were married?"

"Uh-huh," Martha sounded in agreement. "Nice, huh?"

"Thanks for suggesting we do this," Craig said as he smoothed a lock of her hair that had been dislodged by the breeze that had picked up a bit. He softly continued speaking, "In a couple of months, we have to make a decision about what comes next. Do I run for sheriff again or do I hang it up?"

"Did one of those Horney toads crawl up your pant leg? What's this "we" thing. You do what you do because you love it and you need to make that decision."

"While you've been waging this battle, having the surgery then going through recovery, and now the radiation treatments I realize how selfish I've been, not spending more time with you."

"Craig, you love what you do, few people can say that about what they do to make a living. Yes, I'll admit that over the years, I've spent some sleepless nights while you're out chasing some crazy, wondering if you will come home in one piece or worst, but you are good at what you do. The evidence is that you've served the people of the county for five terms, four uncontested." She paused and positioned herself so she could look him in the eye. "Because of the time you've spent with me, from you, I've drawn the strength to fight through the tough times. So, don't beat yourself up because you're there more often." Again, she paused. "If you feel it's time to let someone else do this job, you do it. If you're not ready to take off that badge, I'll support you as I always have. But this is a decision that I won't help you make."

They sat quietly with their arms around one another for a long time, neither of them spoke, but both contemplating the next chapter in their lives. They sat and watched the sun go down. It was a typical Wyoming sunset; a collage of yellow, oranges, and reds across the evening sky and reflected in the rippling waters of the Green River.

The night birds were out, diving and flittering up and down, performing chandelles in pursuit of and catching flying insects that were now reclaiming the park. Craig stood and extended both arms to help Martha to her feet.

"Come," he said as she rose. "We'll stop by Baskin Robins and I'll buy your favorite flavored ice cream to cap off a perfect day."

"You sure know how to impress a girl," Martha said as they strolled across the grass hand in hand.

The next few weeks were pretty routine. The most excitement was at the emergency detention lockup rooms at the hospital. There was the man found by the highway patrol late at night, wandering in the median on I-80. He was incoherent, confused, and combative. The officers determined that he was a danger to himself and others, thus, he was detained against his will.

*****

It was early morning when Fred and Amy Dreskel got the call and they decided that they'd begin their inspection of the guards at client facilities at the hospital. They assumed they'd only be there a couple of hours at the most. Up on their arrival, they learned that the detainee's name was Tony Olano, a truck driver. During the length of time it took to process him into the hospital, he had become less confused. But he couldn't remember where he'd left his truck. He smelled awful.

"When's the last time you've had a shower?" Fred asked. "You smell terrible."

"Been about a week," Tony responded. "If the lady will be so kind as to step out I'd like to show you something."

Amy was only too happy to oblige. She went into the hallway and began calling guard personnel that were on standby to guard people that were in lockup. Tony opened the hospital gown he'd been given and showed Fred the upper thigh on his left leg. Fred fought to keep from puking. A large area was raw and resembled hamburger in appearance. An open sore with little beads of yellow puss, oozing out of it, and it smelled.

"I haven't been able to wash myself because of this and it hurts like hell. I've been taking pain killers for the past few days, trying to kill the pain, and deliver my load to Salt Lake City. I don't really remember much about how I got here, I just came to myself down in the emergency room with a bunch of cops around me. Sure could use something for the pain right now."

"We'll have to wait for the doctor to come by before you can get anything for the pain, in the meantime, we've got to get you and that wound cleaned up," Fred advised him as he left the room.

At the nurse's station, Fred explained what he had to the charge nurse. She took some gloves from a box under the station's counter and followed Fred back to the room.

"Mr. Olano, I understand you have an ouch on your leg. May I see it?"

Fred watched as the nurse tenderly probed the boundaries of the sore and Tony winch each time she touched it.

She stepped back and asked Fred to follow her out of the room. In the hallway, she explained what needed to be done. "We have to get him cleaned up, then we need to clean that sore. If I make a protective patch for that sore, can you people give him a shower? I'll get you some protective clothing and soft brushes. I'm not sure what we've got here. I'll put a call in to the doctor assigned this floor and have him take a look."

"Sure," Fred responded. "Whatever we can do help."

The doctor responded rather quickly after the nurse made the call. After the nurse explained the situation, he had Tony lay back on his bed exposing his leg with the sore.

"How long have you had this?" the doctor asked.

"About a week," Tony responded.

"You been doing anything for it?" the doctor continued to probe.

"Just taking pain pills."

"What have you been taking?"

"Aleve, ibuprofen, and aspirin mostly."

"Mostly?" the doctor asked. "Did you take something else?"

"I got some pills from another trucker yesterday. He said they would knock any kind of pain."

"You know what they were?"

"No. Didn't ask. I just wanted the pain to stop."

"We're going to draw some blood and run some test, but I think we've got a case of shingles that has become infected. See if you can get him cleaned up, protect that area so that no dirty water gets in it, then clean that area with some soap and cool water. We'll administer some antibiotics through an IV once he's all cleaned up."

As the doctor prepared to leave, Tony took his arm. "Can I get something for the pain, Doc?"

"We'll keep placing cool pads on that area until I get the test results back. The cool pads will help reduce the pain some and the itching. I think once we get the infection under control, you won't be as uncomfortable."

After the doctor was gone, the nurse returned from her station with some saran wrap, with which she gently covered the sore area and secured it with medical tape. The shower was just across the hall. Fred and Amy still put on the protective clothing so that they didn't get wet as they washed Tony from head to toe, avoiding the covered area on his upper thigh.

When Tony was all clean, the nurse returned. She had a spray bottle of soapy water and some pads that she used to clean the area affected by the shingles. When she finished cleaning the area, she put a light coat of an ointment over it and cautioned Tony about rubbing or scratching.

Amy came into the room just as the nurse was finishing up and announced that the highway patrol had located Tony's truck. It was parked at a rest stop about three miles from where he was picked up. "Your company has been notified and they are making arrangements to take care of the truck and the cargo," Amy said. "Which, by the way, was not at all happy according to the patrol officers."

"What did they mean?" Fred inquired.

"Tony was transporting beef on the hoof, about thirty head. A local rancher is caring for them," Amy explained.

*****

The next few weeks were uneventful, but for a steady commitment of persons to the emergency detention facility at the hospital. Attempted suicides, overdoses, persons in need of stabilization because they stopped taking prescribed medications, were generally the reasons for the interments. Fred and Amy Driskell were extremely busy while there was a relative lull in activity at the sheriff's department. There was one instance of excitement which occurred while Craig was having lunch one day.

Martha had made ham and tomato sandwiches and Craig was halfway through his when the phone rang. Martha answered it and handed the phone to Craig. "It's dispatch," she informed him.

"Yeh, dispatch, what's up?" Craig asked.

"Sheriff, sorry to bother you but it is essential that you meet SO2 at your office asap."

"10-4," Craig responded. He took a big bite out of the last half of his sandwich as he stood to leave.

"Should have known things were too quiet around here. Gotta run, doll, thanks for lunch," he said to Martha as he gave her a kiss on the forehead.

As he crossed the street and entered the courthouse, Craig tried to imagine what could be so urgent. Did something happen in the jail? Surely, we don't have another killing on our hands, he hoped, or an escape. By the time he reached his office, he was out of breath.

When he opened the door to his office, Steve, Lolly, Kevin, Fred, and Amy Driskell along, with Sister Mary Margaret, were standing like soldiers all in a line. They seemed to be shielding someone seated behind them but Craig couldn't see who it was. Mary Margret spoke first. "Sheriff Spence, I'm sure you never expected to see me again and were it not for necessary travel, that may have been so. We have an appointment in Salt Lake City later this afternoon and have a few minutes to spare. Someone that feels indebted to you and your associates insisted that we stop by so that she could thank you in person. I understand that the two of you have never actually met, so, Sheriff, let me introduce you to Sister Patricia Anne."

The group stepped aside and sitting behind them was a young lady, wearing a blue turbine type wrap on her head. Her face pale and a slight crooked smile on her lips. With the help of two canes, she rose rather unsteadily to her feet. Slowly, she put one foot in front of the other and made her way to where Craig was standing, still trying to catch his breath. Craig removed his hat and held it at his side, as Sister Patricia Anne began to speak, haltingly, her words very deliberate and slightly slurred. "But for the grace of God, your staff, and talented surgeons, I'm able to stand before you and express my gratitude. Because of you people, I am alive with a second chance to do God's work. Thank you."

Craig reached out and took her in his arms saying, "May the good Lord continue to bless you, Sister."

While Craig and Sister Patricia Anne embraced, the office door opened and Joyce, the security officer that spent the most time with Patricia Anne, entered the room. "Sorry I'm late. I hit every red light in town I—" Joyce stopped midsentence as she recognized who Craig was holding.

Patricia Anne disengaged herself from Craig's embrace and moved toward Joyce who stood some distance from the group. Neither of them spoke as Patricia Anne took Joyce's face in her hands. Both canes fell to the floor and Joyce put her arms under the Sister's elbows to lend support.

"I remember you," Patricia Anne said. "Not your name but your face. You were kind to me. You helped me when I couldn't help myself. Thank you so very much."

The tears ran down both their faces. Joyce's through the fingers of Patricia Anne's hands, and Patricia Anne's dampened Joyce's blouse as they now stood very close, Patricia still holding Joyce's face.

"Surely you are a miracle!" Joyce exclaimed. "I never thought I'd ever see you again."

There were sniffles being heard among the rest of the group also but it was Sister Mary Margret that broke the spell as she and Steve picked up the canes and handed them to Patricia. "We have some distance to travel, so we must be on our way. Your gathering here on such short notice is much appreciated. You've made Sister Patricia Anne very happy. We'll be taking our leave now. God willing, our paths will cross again."

Kevin held the door and they all watched as the two Sisters slowly made their way down the hall to the building's lobby.

CHAPTER 11

The lull in activity at the Sweetwater County sheriff's office was destined to be short-lived and the entire law enforcement community would be impacted by coming events that were the result of actions taken months prior.

Around the first of the year, Matt Kessler, chief of the Rock Springs PD, under pressure from members of the city council, came up with a plan to crack down on prostitution and gambling which was again becoming a source of citizen complaints and from which other criminal enterprises manifested themselves. Using the insistence of the council that increased enforcement measures be directed at the problem, Matt easily gained approval to transfer funds from the department's transportation budget to pay for a temporary undercover position. Since all the officers currently on the force were well known, Matt's plan was to bring someone on from another location to infiltrate and/or help develop cases against those engaged in specific operations.

Having worked with undercover personnel of several departments in other states, Matt contacted them directly in an attempt perhaps to broker a loan arrangement. He was in luck. One of the departments feared that their undercover guy had been compromised and jumped at the opportunity to hide him for a period.

After transfer arrangements were completed, Marty Keyster, a small man with long stringy black hair, sporting a goatee that made him look like Lucifer, and wearing granny glasses, met Matt and his lead detective Cleve "Pappy" Masters at the Laramie Police Department. Marty was from Illinois and had a cocky air about him. His eyes were bloodshot and Pappy detected the odor of marijuana. When Marty left the room to use the rest room, Pappy had expressed misgivings to Matt who reminded him that Marty was expected to do a job that required a special type.

When Marty returned, he started the conversation. "I understand what you are trying to do," Marty said. "I can do the job. I'm the best at this stuff."

"If you're the best, how did you get found out?" Pappy asked, not impressed at all.

"I'm going through a divorce. My wife tried to set me up by putting out the word that I was a NARC," Marty responded.

"How do you know it was your wife?" Matt had inquired.

"One of my prostitute informants gave me a heads-up, but that's then, let's talk about now." Marty had leaned forward in his chair and had spoken directly to Matt. "If you want me to do this job, you two are the only ones who know who and what I am. I'll undoubtedly be arrested at some point by your people. Stay out of it, I'll get out on my own. My contact will be you." He was speaking to Cleve. "What did you say your name was?" Marty asked Pappy with sarcasm in his tone.

"Everyone calls me Pappy, you can call me Mr. Masters."

"Okay, I'll probably show up in your town in a couple of days. I'll spread the word around town that my moniker is MK, who may have drug connections. When I've got something, I'll get a message to you, *Mr. Masters.*"

With that, Marty had gotten up, pulled a knitted cap out of his hip pocket, pulled it down over his ears and gave one last glance at Pappy as he walked out of the interrogation room that they had been allowed to use.

"I've got a bad feeling about that guy, Chief," Pappy had commented.

"I'm not thrilled either," Matt had assured Pappy. "Right now, he's all we got. Let's see how it goes . . ."

Matt knew that most of the illicit activity seemed to be centered around a prominent night spot north of town called the Silver Dollar. It had been an old warehouse that the local sheep industry had used to process wool, hold auctions, and the point from which wool was shipped to clothing manufacturers back east. A group out of Denver had purchased the place, completely renovated the interior and setup a high-end restaurant, a bar, and dance hall that also included a pool parlor and game room. Business was good any night of the week and overflowing on weekends. Matt and his detectives had tried, on several occasions, to catch the management operating or allowing gambling to no avail. On one occasion, the county judge had authorized a search warrant on information that a bevy of out of town prostitutes were going to be working the club on a weekend. The only thing found was two bedrooms that were used by managers who worked through the wee hours of the morning. The managers had personal belongings in the rooms which gave legitimacy to the bedrooms being there. Shirts and blouses with names embroidered on the pockets; a handbag with deposit slips and receipts bearing the name of a person employed at the time as a hostess at the restaurant; a card holder on a dresser in one of the rooms with credit cards and driver's license of the general manager. The place had been full of locals, a few of the towns regular bar hoppers but none of the circuit crowed as had been purported. The department had been setup by a very unreliable informant or the raid had not been kept a secret.

Matt had become rather nervous when there had been no contact from Marty after three weeks had passed. The embarrassment of the failed, poorly planned raid was encouragement enough to cause him to be patient, even though Pappy Masters had constantly reminded him of his discomfort with the situation.

Finally, just short of a month, a letter arrived at the police department addressed to Chief of Police, Rock Springs Police Department—Attention: Mr. Masters. The letter was certified and a signature was required. The letter had been sent from the Ft. Collins, Colorado Police Department. Since the letter had been addressed to the chief of police, Matt decided to open it and then pass it on to Pappy. He advised his secretary that he didn't want to be disturbed, closed his office door, and sat down at his desk. Taking a letter opener from the desk's center drawer, he slit the envelope open and took out several sheets of paper with typewritten text.

"Chief, Matt," the letter began. "Surprised? Me too, when I found out that the locals already knew that there was a plant in town. Let me tell you a story."

Matt stopped reading and took a highlighter and highlighted in yellow the part about the locals knowing about a plant, then he continued reading.

"I got in town a couple of days after I talked to you," Marty wrote on. "For three nights, I hung out at the bar in the Silver Dollar. Was making some jazz with a big, good-looking blonde bartender. She seemed to have a handle on things. She pointed out people that I had to get to know if I wanted to be treated right. On the third night, while I was having a totty and we were jawin, a bald-headed guy, weight lifter type, walked behind the bar, took a set of keys, and locked the cash register. He turned to the barkeep, stuck his finger right between her tits, and told her that he had been watching her and figured she had stiffed the place for over five hundred in the last two weeks. Without taking a breath, and as he kept stabbing her in the chest with that finger, he told her to get her fat ass out and not to come back. I'm telling you all this because you might be able to use the info later. Right now, from what I learned in those three days I don't think you guys could catch a grasshopper with a fishing net."

Matt highlighted Marty's descriptions of the guy and the bartender. He re-read the part about the grasshopper and a scowl crossed his face and he didn't highlight that part. He read on.

"That bartender was some kinda pissed. She called that guy names I never heard before, as he was pushing her out the door. I know better than to hit a gift horse in the mouth, so I followed her across the street to the Three Amigos Hotel. She went straight to the hotel bar and after she had ordered a drink, I took a stool next to her. She was ready to talk and she had a story to tell. She said that prostitutes come into town from Utah or Colorado every weekend. They were in town the night you pulled the raid. The reason your raid wasn't successful was the management at the Silver Dollar had a heads-up. They knew you were coming. They moved the operation over to the Three Amigos Hotel that night. It worked out so well that every weekend since, they get a block of rooms and the ladies function undisturbed. She blew me away when she told me the Dollar had someone at the PD in their pocket, and they knew every move the cops made. That's how they knew that there was a plant. Me being new in town, I figured they'd be looking at me so, I put some distance between me and your town. There's only three of us that knew about the gig and it wasn't me that got diarrhea of the mouth. I got a feeling you didn't flap your lips either, see where I'm going? Good luck, Chief, I'm sitting this one out." The letter was signed, Marty.

Matt re-read that portion of the letter where Marty visited with the girl in the bar, and highlighted most of it to the letter's end. He sat back in his chair and stared for a long time at those sheets of paper on his desk. The longer he contemplated what was being implicated in the letter, the more trouble he had imagining that Pappy would be involved in anything of this sort. *There was no one on the force that was more trustworthy than Pappy,* he thought.

Matt folded the letter and put it in the center drawer of his desk and locked it. He wanted to think this through and talk to his good friend, Craig Spence, before making any moves. He pushed the blue button on his phone, which connected him directly to his dispatch center.

"Yes, Chief," came an instant response.

"See if you can run down Sheriff Spence and patch him through on my secure line," Matt instructed.

"10-4, Chief." The blue button popped back to its original position and the line to dispatch disconnected.

While he waited, Matt went to his file cabinet that held old reports and pulled out the folder containing reports pertaining to the attempts that had been made to shutdown gambling activities or to catch prostitutes in the act. He personally had never been involved in a raid.

Over the past three months, the reports showed there had been four raids initiated. Each of the raids were based on information provided by one of several informants that members of the detective department had developed.

The Silver Dollar had several banquet rooms. One room was large enough to accommodate small conventions or corporate parties. There were three smaller rooms that were used for meetings or private parties. It was one of the smaller rooms, according to informants, that were stripped of the dining setups and replaced with poker and black jack tables when they ran their gambling operations.

Matt noticed that Pappy Masters had been in charge of each of the raids. Only one raid was conducted with a search warrant. The others were conducted with the permission of the proprietor. On each raid, Pappy had used two patrolmen and two of his detectives. None of the patrolmen were used more than once, but one of the detectives participated in each raid, a female by the name of Cathy Prator. Matt understood why Pappy would use a female. There's always the probability that at least one female would be swept up in a raid and it was prudent to have a female officer handle her. The phone rang, it was his direct line.

"This is Chief Kessler," he answered.

"Spence here, Chief, haven't talked with you since we lost that prisoner back a ways, good to hear from ya."

"Yeh, Craig, looks like the only time we talk is when one of us is in trouble."

"I'm not in trouble, Matt, but I've had it on my to-do list to call ya, tell me, what can I do for ya?"

"I have a situation that I want to run by you to see if you might have some suggestions about how I should handle it," Matt confided.

"City council tightening the screws again, are they?" Craig assumed that Matt was battling for his department's survival, as usual.

"No, it's more serious than that," Matt replied.

"Okay, your place or mine," Craig inquired.

"I need to get out of the city, why don't we meet at Mamma Bessie's for lunch tomorrow?" Matt thought that was a great suggestion.

"Deal," Craig agreed. "See you there around 11:30?"

"You buying?" Matt asked.

"Flip you for it. You flip a quarter. I'll pick heads or tail. I trust ya," Craig countered.

"Okay," Matt replied. There was a short pause before he continued. "It's tails," he said.

"That's just what I picked," Craig said through a giggle. "You're buying."

Mamma Bessie's was a restaurant located halfway between Rock Springs and Green River, on the south side of I-80. The restaurant was owned by the matriarch of one of the few black families in the county. Ms. Bess was in her early eighties, she opened her restaurant two days a week. She did all the cooking, she had one waitress who doubled as the custodian. On the days the restaurant was open, people stood in line to get one of the eight tables.

Craig arrived at the restaurant first. As soon as Ms. Bess saw him, she came out of her kitchen and gave him a hug. She had voted for him every time he ran.

"Hello, boyfriend of mine," she said through a big toothless smile.

"Hi-ya, Bess! You're still my best girl," Craig said as he gave her a gentle squeeze.

"What brings you to my place?" Bess asked.

"I'm meeting Chief Kessler here," Craig answered.

"God bless!" Exclaimed Bess. "Two top cops in my place at the same time. People gonna think Bess is in a heap of trouble." Both chuckled as she led Craig to an empty table. Craig had just gotten settled in his seat when Matt pulled out a chair and sat down. The two of them exchanged pleasantries, placed their lunch order, and while waiting, Matt briefed Craig about his situation.

"Craig, we at the department have been trying to corral the prostitutes that have started coming to town again and put a stop to the gambling activities that have sprung up. We weren't having any luck so I borrowed an undercover guy from one of the departments in

Colorado, thinking that an unknown might be able to give us a lead as to what's going on."

"You mean, that little guy with straight black hair and goatee that hung out at the Silver Dollar for a couple of days was your guy?" Craig asked.

Matt responded with surprise in his voice, "Yeh, how did you know about him?"

"I guess I owe you an apology, Matt. We've had a man inside the Silver Dollar for a month now. He works for the security company we contract with. Should have coordinated with you, I guess. He spotted your guy the first night he showed up. Nobody wears that type of goatee around here, he stood out like a sore thumb," Craig confessed.

"Somebody put the word out that there was a plant. Was it your guy that did that?" Matt asked.

"Maybe, don't know for sure," Craig responded. "By the way, been meaning to call you and ask you about one of your people that's frequently in the place."

The food arrived and Craig stopped his inquiry. Matt, too, sat quietly while their food was being placed in front of them. When the waitress left, Matt queried Craig, "What's this about one of my people?"

"There is a female," Craig began, "blonde haired, about five six five seven. According to our guy, she generally comes in wearing street cloths, but a couple of times she has been in uniform. Our man caught a glimpse of her name tag and saw Melisa, didn't get the last name, goes straight to the manager's office like she's one of the staff. A couple of times, in the evening, she has sat at the end of the bar and chatted with the bartender. At first, we thought she might be moonlighting as security or something, but now we think not. You know what's with her, Matt?"

"Sounds like Melisa Odom," Matt started. "She's one of our detectives. I haven't authorized anyone to moonlight at the Silver Dollar, but I don't concern myself about what they do off duty as long as they don't violate policy or procedures or reflect negatively upon the department or the city."

"Well," Craig began. "For your information, we are planning to bust the gambling operation at the Silver Dollar this coming weekend. We don't have anything on the prostitution operations." Matt leaned forward in his seat and spoke quietly, "The one thing we did learn from our guy with the goatee, is how and where they conduct that operation, but I've got that problem."

"I would bet my bottom dollar that Pappy is not your snitch," Craig said. "I've known him since he came to town. I was in my second term. He's honest and a good cop. Who is present during your planning sessions?"

Matt thought for a minute. "Well, there's myself, there's Pappy, and his crew. He only has four detectives, one being Melisa Odom, then there is the dispatcher that is scheduled to be on duty the day or night of the raid."

"Okay," Craig said, as he scratched his head. "Pappy uses the same people each time, how about the dispatcher?"

"Don Perkins," Matt recalled as he sat back in his seat. "When he applied for the job, he was working at the Silver Dollar as their night auditor. You mean the bastard is right under my nose?"

"There's one way to find out," Craig said. "Plan a dummy raid to take place the following weekend, so you'll have to have your meeting no earlier than the day before. That way you put the squeeze on and whomever it is will have to get the word out in a hurry. Make sure you have your secretary type up a request for a search warrant so everything will look on the up and up. Don't let Pappy in on it. I'm sure he's not your man, but I could be wrong. I'll even have one of my troops set in on the meeting as if we're supporting the operation. Have Pappy only bring two of his people to the planning meeting, Melisa and one other. Whoever it is, is not going to contact anyone using the department phones because they're all hooked up to your recorder. They will have to make contact outside of the building. That's where your other two dicks come in. Have one keep tabs on the dispatcher and the other cover Melisa. You'll know by night fall who your snitch is."

"Craig Spence, you're a devious old cuss," Matt whispered to Craig. "Damned if I don't believe it will work."

"If it don't, I'll buy you lunch next time." Craig stood up and adjusted his hat. "Gotta go, let me know when you're holding that meeting," he said, patting Matt on the back and Matt flipped the brim of Craig's hat, cocking it to one side.

The meeting went off just as Craig and Matt had planned. Matt had a detailed outline as to how things would go down. Everyone knew exactly what their job was and the sheriff's deputies were to cover the outside, front and back, of the Three Amigos Hotel to pick up any of the ladies that may slip out. Matt had everyone go over the details several times just like they would for any such raid.

After the meeting, Matt called in the two detectives that would normally work the night shift and laid out the plan and the objective. It was close to lunch time, so they had time to setup and observe their targets as they went to lunch.

Melisa was working the eight to four shift and always had her lunch at the Silver Dollar restaurant that opened at 11:30 a.m. every day. She generally had a luncheon partner, a middle-aged woman, neatly dressed and always had a pencil stuck in her hair over the right ear. Today was no different. The woman was observed entering the dining area from a hallway that led to the restrooms, she walked past the detective who had taken a seat at that end of the lunch counter. From where he was seated, display cases for pastry and the cash register made it difficult for Melisa to see him. The woman walked to a corner table where Melisa was sitting, gave her a hug and sat down. The detective slipped off his stool and walked down the hallway to the men's room. A door at the end of the hall had a sign that read: "authorized persons only" and in smaller letters, "office manager," leading the detective to assume that the woman had come through that door.

When leaving the men's room, he met Melisa heading to the lady's room.

"Hey, Chuck, "she said, as she pointed in the direction of the table where she had been sitting. "I'm siting over there, why don't you come join us?"

Chuck was not disappointed that he had been seen. He wanted to know who this woman sitting with Melisa was anyway, and since he wasn't expected to be working, what a neat way to keep an eye on Melisa and get a feel for what she's up to. As he approached the table, the woman looked up with a questioning expression on her face so he introduced himself. "Hi, I'm Chuck. I work with Melisa, she invited me over."

"Oh, Hi, I'm Kate. I'm Melisa's roommate and the office manager for the restaurant."

"Boy," Chuck responded. "It must really be a tough job keeping track of all the activities in this complex, huh?"

"Oh no," Kate said. "I just supervise the restaurant portion of things. I don't have any idea what goes on in the rest of the place."

"You two introduce yourselves?" Melisa asked as she re-joined them at the table.

*****

Don Perkins was relieved for lunch by the shift commander. He lived in a mobile home park, on the city's east side about four miles from city hall, rode a motor cycle to work, and generally went home for lunch.

Troy Mechum, the detective assigned to observe was parked a block away from city hall when Don left for lunch. Instead of taking the street that would take him east of town, he headed west. Troy followed at some distance to College Hill where many of the business people owned homes. Don pulled up to a mail box and put something in it, he then sped off and took I-80 to the east. Troy took an envelope from the mail box, stuck in his shirt pocket, jotted down the address and followed Don to his house.

Matt had brown bagged it today. His wife had fixed him a couple of brisket sandwiches, threw in a bag of chips, and some chocolate chip cookies. He had gotten a Dr. Pepper from the machine in the break room and was enjoying his lunch, when there as a knock on his office door.

"Enter," Matt shouted out.

A young man in blue coveralls walked in. It was the city radio and communications technician. "Hi, Chief," he said.

"Hello there," Matt responded.

"Chief, I was servicing the recording system and switching out the reels. While I ate my lunch, I played back a section of the reel I was switching out to check out the quality when I heard something I think you ought to come hear."

Matt left his office with the technician and walked down to the communications center which was located where the dispatchers work. Once inside, the technician took out a notepad and described what he had.

"I played back a portion of this morning's recordings," he said. "From number 342607 to number 342610 is what I want you to hear."

"Okay," Matt said. "Let er rip."

The technician flipped a switch and a phone could be heard ringing. There were three rings and then the phone was answered. "Silver Dollar, this is George, how can I help you?" Then a female voice said, "Raid, 10:30 PM, tomorrow night." There was a click and then silence. Matt sat stone-faced.

"Play that again," Matt requested.

The technician complied.

"That's Maggie!" Matt exclaimed. "That's Maggie, my secretary!"

*****

The detectives that were assigned to tail Melisa Odom and Don Perkins reported what they had observed to Pappy Masters. He, in turn, reported to Matt. He gave the envelope that Troy had picked up to Matt, still unopened.

"The raid is off," Matt told Pappy and told him to pass the word to his people.

"What's up, Chief?" His chief of detectives asked.

"Don't ask," Matt replied. "Do me a favor, and let everybody know that the raid's off."

After Pappy had left his office, Matt sat for a while, trying to understand what had happened. The big question—why? Why did she do it? He opened the envelope that Troy had picked up. When he read the message inside, he couldn't help but burst in to a fit of laughter. The message read, "Can't make it to dinner tomorrow. Have to work."

At 4:30 p.m., Matt punched the intercom button to Maggie's office. "Maggie, would you step into my office please." He didn't wait for an answer, he hung up. The door to his office opened and Maggie, pad in hand, entered and sat in a chair beside Matt's desk.

"You want to tell me before or after I fire you?" His voice was hard and cold. He stared directly into her eyes. Maggie choked up, her body shaking as the sobs she tried to hold back got away. She dropped the pad and covered her face with her hands. Matt just waited, steel-faced with anger in his eyes. Then he spoke. "I trusted you, Maggie," his voice softened a little. "You owe me an explanation," he demanded as he extracted a box of tissues from a lower desk drawer.

After wiping away the tears and blowing her nose, Maggie apologized profusely. "Matt, I would never betray you in any way, I love my job and I love working for you, but I was forced and I didn't know what to do," Maggie said and the sobs started again. Matt just waited until she started once more. "My husband," she began. "My husband gambled at the Silver Dollar and lost a lot of money. More money than we could ever repay. They beat him and told him that they were going to make him disappear. When we couldn't come up with the money, they came to the house and threatened to make me prostitute myself until we'd paid the money back. When they found out that I worked here, they said they'd make me a deal. If I'd tell them what the police were planning, they'd let us payoff the debt that way. I didn't know what to do. I'm so sorry," and the tears flowed and her chest heaved as she sobbed uncontrollably.

"Why didn't you come to me?" Matt asked.

"I was scared. I was ashamed. I didn't want to lose my job, and I didn't want to be a prostitute. I didn't know what to do."

Matt got out of his chair and turned to look out the window behind his desk. He was feeling multiple emotions all at the same time—disappointment, frustration, regret, anger, and sorrow. He could hear Maggie sobbing behind him. Finally, he turned to face her. "You don't talk to anyone about this," he said in a stern voice. "When you get home, you let them know that the raid has been called off because we couldn't muster enough bodies. You be at your desk early in the morning. We've got a lot of work to do.

The end